MUR
THE MANOR

A gripping crime mystery with a killer twist

ANNE PENKETH

DI Clayton Mystery Book 4

JOFFE BOOKS

Joffe Books, London
www.joffebooks.com

First published in Great Britain in 2021

This book is a work of fiction. Names, characters, businesses, organizations, places and events are either the product of the author's imagination or are used fictitiously. Any resemblance to actual persons, living or dead, events or locales is entirely coincidental. The spelling used is British English except where fidelity to the author's rendering of accent or dialect supersedes this.

Cover art by Dee Dee Book Covers

ISBN: 978-1-78931-927-9

To the Silent Zoomers, Carola, Christine, Rik and Sarah,
my writing companions in lockdown

CHAPTER ONE

Dennis Iverson allowed himself a smile of satisfaction as he greeted the guests arriving for his son's fancy-dress party.

He could have thrown himself into the role of lord of the manor, but this was Rupert's night, and he didn't want to overstay his welcome. That was why he was the only one not in costume — he was wearing a suit for the occasion. He didn't need to introduce himself, really. Everyone knew that he was the owner of Iverson Hall, in the village where he'd started out as a brickie.

He felt a raindrop on his forehead and looked up at the scudding clouds in the September sky. He rubbed his greying beard and stepped back into the porch. Would the weather cooperate? He didn't want anything to spoil the birthday party.

Rupert was his youngest, the apple of his father's eye. Dennis could hear his distinctive "haw, haw" laugh in the hall behind him. He turned round and spotted his son in the centre of a group of women who were helping themselves to the drinks and nibbles being handed round by the catering staff. The women were dressed in ornate gowns and wigs, and some were masked. He had no idea who any of them were. But then, you're only twenty-five once, he thought. That was why he'd offered to pay for the festivities. Little had he known that Rupert would invite twenty-four of his closest friends to dress up for 'The Court of the Sun King'. With Rupert in the role of Louis XIV, of course. God knows why they'd picked that particular theme.

Rupert himself was a slender man, tanned from his outdoor life, but his appearance had been transformed by a black wig, the curls tumbling onto his burgundy satin jacket. The Louis XIV look was completed by thick white stockings and heeled red shoes.

The twang of a harpsichord was almost drowned out by the buzz of conversation. Ah well, thought Dennis, this would probably be one of the last family parties at the manor. One by one, the houses nearby were slipping into the sea as the crashing waves burrowed into the cliffs. Although set further back than some, Iverson Hall was edging ever closer to the drop. How much longer could it survive?

He loved the solid elegance of the Georgian house, with its spacious reception rooms, landscaped garden and sweeping views towards the sea from the upper floors. Yet its terminal fragility was now exposed. It would be a tragedy when the inevitable happened. The sea seemed to be encroaching ever faster, forcing villagers out of their homes. After failing to find a buyer some years earlier, Dennis had decided to rent the manor out as a party house, which had been a very lucrative endeavour marred only by the complaints from neighbours about the noise — Iverson Hall was popular with guests who liked to party hard. He'd personally posted notes through the letterboxes of all the neighbours to let them know about Rupert's birthday celebration. Surely they wouldn't begrudge him that? He'd never met such a bunch of miserable wretches.

A red Jag was creeping along the drive under the holm oaks, where other guests had already parked on either side. As the car came to a halt, Dennis went out to talk to the driver.

"Terribly sorry, but you'll have to turn back and find somewhere round the corner," he said.

"Hello, Mr Iverson, it's me, Bethany. We'll jump out here," a young woman in a flowing blue dress called out from the back. Chocolate-coloured ringlets descended onto her cheeks. Could they be real? He remembered Bethany as a redhead.

A delicate ankle and a ribbon-tied heeled shoe emerged from under the car door. Dennis went to help her get out of the car in her flounced costume. She reached inside for a designer bag while her escort stepped out from the other side dressed in a long velvet jacket over brocade knee breeches. The Jag, free of passengers, began a complicated turn outside the house. Dennis's own gleaming Rolls had pride of place on the gravel.

"Welcome to Versailles-on-Sea." Dennis performed an exaggerated bow. He took her hand and bent over as he raised it to his lips in a baisemain. He'd always liked Rupert's ex-girlfriend.

She appeared charmed.

"This is fun, isn't it?" she exclaimed. She indicated her surly companion. "Do you know Jacob?"

"Indeed I do." Dennis wasn't actually sure that they'd met. He remembered being told that the boyfriend commuted to work in the City.

Bethany, like Rupert, had studied architecture in London. If they'd played their cards right, they could both have joined him in the family building firm. But to Dennis's dismay, Bethany had walked out on Rupert before their finals, prompting him to return to Norfolk to nurse a broken heart, never completing his degree. Bethany had gone on to work in town planning in Norwich, according to what he'd heard from Rupert.

Dennis lit a cigarette. He watched Bethany and Rupert embrace in the hall under a glittering chandelier, his son touching her on the arm while she talked animatedly. The boyfriend waited for her at a discreet distance.

He still felt protective of Rupert, who'd never really got it together after the split from Bethany. He had a smallholding in the village, a far cry from the brilliant career in the family firm that his father had anticipated for him. Everyone knew Iverson and Son around here, but the 'Son' referred to Dennis's eldest, Jeremy. He wasn't here tonight, which surprised nobody. The two brothers weren't close.

Dennis leaned against the solid front door and looked around the spacious hall. Every nook and cranny held memories of the time when the manor had been their family home. What would the future hold? he wondered.

The guests were milling around, beginning to explore the rest of the house with drinks in hand. Some of them would be staying the night. A small bewigged blonde in a cascading red dress approached Rupert and dragged him away from Bethany. That was Cathy, Rupert's current girlfriend, who worked on a local dairy farm and now lived with Rupert on the smallholding — the rent and various outgoings paid for by Dennis. And Cathy was nice enough, but . . . she wasn't Bethany. Dennis allowed himself a little sigh.

Surely everyone must be here now? He checked his watch. It was 9.30 p.m. The invitations had said 8.30 for 9 p.m. With a final glance behind him, and after failing to catch Rupert's eye to say goodnight, Dennis stubbed out his cigarette on the gravel, climbed into the Rolls and drove home to Norwich.

CHAPTER TWO

"So what do we know about Tideburgh?" DI Sam Clayton asked DS Julie Everett, who was sitting beside him in the car. They'd been sent to the village after local police contacted Anglian Constabulary to report a suspicious death. As far as they were both concerned, it was a rare sunny day and another Sunday ruined.

"Apart from how to pronounce it," he added.

Julie, who was originally from Ipswich, had already had to correct Clayton's pronunciation of the village known locally as *Tid-bruh*. Even after all this time, she thought, Clayton still didn't seem at home in Norfolk. Whenever they drove out to a case on the North Norfolk coast, he'd complain about the flatness compared to the fells of his native Lancashire.

"It's so bloody flat round here, isn't it?" he said on cue as they approached Wroxham. Julie ignored him. He probably didn't expect an answer anyway.

"Sometimes it's like we're in a foreign country, with the way they pronounce all these names," he grumbled. "I mean, Wymondham, Cley, Stiffkey . . . why can't they spell them so everyone knows how to pronounce them?"

Julie looked up from her phone on which she was reading a potted history of the village. They came to a stop behind the traffic waiting to go over the bridge with its views of the boats docked along the River Bure.

"I bet it's not like that up north," she said with a smile.

"Of course not." She watched as he tapped his fingers on the steering wheel, possibly regretting his firm denial. The car juddered forwards, passing customers who were filing into Roy's department store on the other side of the bridge.

"Well, only the odd one," he said. "Anyway, what does it say about Tideburgh in there?"

"Let's see. I went to the village next to Tideburgh on holiday with my parents once when I was a kid. It's spelled Happisburgh but everyone pronounces it as *Haze-bruh*."

"Of course," Clayton interjected.

"The only thing I can remember is the lighthouse, building sandcastles and eating fish and chips on the caravan site. I read that they had to move the whole site inland because of the collapsing cliffs."

"But what does it say about Tideburgh?"

"Not much, actually. There's a cross-reference to Happisburgh, which is of more historic interest. But it says the manor house in Tideburgh is haunted." She glanced across at Clayton. "And that's where we're going."

"Come on, Julie, not another ghost story." He was only half joking. Julie remembered Clayton's scepticism from an earlier murder case involving a clairvoyant, when he'd mocked her intuition. Unfairly, as it turned out.

"No, listen, it's a bit of local history. In the old days there were smugglers in the area and it says the manor house could be built on a smuggler's hoard. And his spirit haunts the house. Apparently." She looked across at him. "Shall I go on?"

She could tell that the answer to that was no. They both laughed.

"Anyway," said Clayton. "As the body was found at the manor house, I think we can assume that this will be a murder investigation about poshos."

Julie had never understood why Clayton had such a big chip on his shoulder. He made such a big deal about his northern working-class roots and the fact that he'd made his way up through the police ranks from school. She'd sensed that his resentment rubbed off on some of his relationships at work, particularly with Dave Bullard, a DC on their team who'd been university intake and was clearly being groomed to zoom. Julie didn't rate Bullard all that highly either but that was mainly because of his sharp elbows and his obsequious manner with DCI Bligh.

She sighed. "Not the kind of poshos you're thinking of. The current owner is a self-made man. A builder. It's his son, Rupert, who was found dead this morning."

"Rupert," said Clayton. "What did I tell you?"

Oh, drop it, Sam, she thought.

Their car turned a corner on a leafy lane. They were still about a mile from Tideburgh.

"Look, there's the Happisburgh lighthouse I was telling you about," Julie called out as the distinctive red-and-white-striped landmark came into view. "Turn right at the T-junction for Tideburgh."

They reached Tideburgh within minutes. The car advanced slowly along the drive leading up to the manor, the oak branches embracing in an arch over their heads. Clayton had to pull over to allow a dark van to pass on its way out.

Julie craned her neck to read the wording on the side. "Caterers. They must have come to collect their stuff. Unfortunately for them, now it's a crime scene."

They approached the house, all three imposing storeys stretched out above them. "Wow," said Clayton. The white stucco facade gleamed in the morning sunlight.

"Isn't it beautiful? Such perfect symmetry."

But Clayton wasn't listening. He'd noticed the white vans parked under the trees to one side while he manoeuvred on the gravel. "The SOCOs are here. You take care of the girlfriend, will you?"

Julie had been expecting that. It was Rupert Iverson's girlfriend who'd raised the alarm earlier that morning. She'd found him floating face down in the pool, still dressed in his Louis XIV costume.

The front door was open, and they made their way inside. Clayton went off to look for the crime scene manager while Julie followed the corridor into a large drawing room where a uniform was sitting on a Chesterfield sofa with a young woman she presumed must be the dead man's partner. Used wine glasses standing on every surface bore witness to the excesses of the night before. Much of the furniture had been pushed back along the walls, presumably to make space for the party.

The policewoman introduced the busty blonde next to her as Cathy Swinson. She looked as though she'd gone to bed straight from the party. She hadn't removed her eye make-up and her tearful cheeks were streaked with black, which gave her a wild and gothic air. She was in jeans and a T-shirt as crumpled as she was.

Julie shook Cathy's ice-cold hand before finding an armchair facing the fireplace to sit on.

"I'm Detective Sergeant Julie Everett. I'm very sorry to hear about Rupert. Can you tell me what happened last night, Cathy?" She took out her notebook. The policewoman got up and signalled that she was leaving.

"It was Rupert's twenty-fifth birthday." Julie noticed that the young woman's accent had the local twang. She was speaking slowly and deliberately. "His dad paid for a fancy-dress party."

"What sort of fancy dress?" Julie asked.

"Rupert described it as 'an invitation to the court of the Sun King'. Louis XIV."

Julie was caught off guard. It sounded rather decadent for such a sleepy village. "Excuse me? Why Louis XIV?"

"Do you remember that TV series *Versailles*? He liked the sex and wigs."

Julie found herself writing down 'sex and wigs' before underlining the words.

"I see," she said. "With Rupert in the role of the king, I presume."

"That's right. I went as his favourite, Madame de Montespan."

"Are you married?"

"He's my boyfriend."

"And when did you notice that he'd gone missing?" Julie asked.

"I woke up in the middle of the night and saw that Rupert wasn't in bed," Cathy replied.

"Did you notice the time?"

"Not really. It must have been about 3 a.m. We went up about two when most of the people had left, and basically crashed out. We were both so tired we couldn't be bothered to take our costumes off. We even kept our wigs on."

"Did anyone else stay the night?"

"Yes. But only two couples. It's a big place," Cathy said, with a small smile. Her speech was halting. "It's got eight bedrooms."

"Are the others still here?"

"I'm afraid they left before I found Rupert. They had to get home for family reasons."

"And what time was that, then?" Julie asked.

Cathy looked at her watch. "They must have gone about ten this morning. Obviously I panicked when Rupert was nowhere to be seen. We searched the whole house, but there was no sign of him." She sighed. "I feel terrible, but we actually had breakfast before I went outside. I said goodbye to our friends. And then . . . there he was, face down in the swimming pool. That's when I called the police. I tried to get him out but he was too heavy. When the ambulance came they said he was already . . . must have been dead long before I found him."

Cathy raised a trembling hand to wipe away mascara from her cheek. Then her whole body convulsed into sobs.

Julie reached out and touched her gently on the arm.

"I'm so sorry, Cathy. Maybe you could give me the details about the other guests. It's important."

Cathy nodded. She identified the two couples who'd stayed overnight as Terry and Karen Monahan, and Brian Mason and Jonathan Murray.

Her lips formed a wan smile. "Brian was hilarious. He came in drag as the king's brother. Do you need the name?" Before Julie could reply, she went on, "Everyone called him Monsieur, but he was Philippe d'Orléans. He was known at the court for dressing in women's clothes, apparently. And Jonathan came as the Chevalier de Lorraine who was Monsieur's lover."

Impressive research, Julie thought, and then remembered it was all probably in the TV show. "Was anyone taking drugs last night?" she asked.

"Some of them might have done. I suppose you'd call it recreational drugs," said Cathy. "There was some laughing gas. But Rupert was clean — he didn't do drugs, I'm sure of it. He doesn't drink, either. I mean, didn't."

"Why do you think that his death is suspicious?" Julie asked.

"It's obvious, isn't it?" she replied. "If he was going for a swim he'd have taken his clothes off, wouldn't he?"

True enough.

"OK. But what if he was drunk, or stumbled?"

"He never drinks! I told you."

"Right. So to recap, you both went up to bed, and then at some point he left the bedroom, fully clothed, and didn't return."

"Yes. Well, at least I guess you could say he didn't, but he might have done because I went back to sleep when I saw he wasn't there. He might have gone to the toilet."

"There was no tension between the two of you?" Julie wondered if Rupert had got up to look for something in particular. *Sex and wigs*, she thought, but didn't voice the question. Cathy was clearly in shock from the morning's discovery.

"No, not really. We'd had our problems like everybody else, but we'd sorted them out." Julie noticed that Cathy was speaking increasingly slowly.

"I see." Julie waited, her pen poised, in case Cathy volunteered anything else about their relationship, but she said nothing more. The moment had passed.

Julie looked round the oak-panelled room and its lavish furnishings. She presumed that the curved sash windows must face the sea.

"Do you live here?" she asked.

"Oh no. These days it's mainly rented out, unless Mr Iverson wants to use it. I live in a place on Vicarage Road with Rupert."

The mention of her partner's name brought on a fresh burst of sobbing. Julie closed her notebook and leaned forward to comfort her.

"I won't keep you, Cathy. But what line of business was Rupert in?"

"We have a smallholding, and we sell organic veggies and chutneys, that sort of thing, at the farmers' market in North Walsham. We're doing really well. Rupert recently managed to get us a contract with a local supermarket. And we're getting ready to sell online too."

At that moment, Julie heard footsteps behind her. Clayton appeared in the doorway with a stocky bearded man in his sixties.

Cathy jumped to her feet and wailed, "Oh, Mr Iverson."

He walked over and gave her an awkward hug. "There, there, Cathy," he said. Julie could see his jaw muscles straining. She wondered about the relations between those two.

Julie stood up and waited for the moment to pass before saying to Cathy, "That's all we need for now." She took out a card and handed it to her. "We'll be in touch," she added, gently. "Let me know if you need anything in the meantime. We can send a family liaison officer if you want."

Cathy nodded, with a vacant air. Julie wondered if she'd taken something to calm herself.

"I'll be off, then," Cathy said like a zombie, and left the room. Clayton introduced Julie before gesturing to Dennis Iverson to take Cathy's place on the sofa.

"We're sorry for your loss," he began.

"He was our youngest." Dennis sank deeper into the sofa and took a cigarette packet out of a pocket. After offering it to them, he lit one and puffed in silence, sending the smoke spiralling into the air. "And now he's gone and never coming back. Who would do this?"

"Maybe you can help us there, sir. The lab report should throw up some clues as well. For example, we should find out whether he was dead before he ended up in the pool," said Clayton. "From what I've been told, it wasn't suicide."

"Suicide? On his birthday? He was a young man who had everything to live for," Dennis retorted. He stubbed out his cigarette and began coughing, a throaty smoker's cough.

Julie asked, "Mr Iverson, would you be able to give us a list of the people who came to the party last night?"

"Yes, of course." Dennis was staring into the middle distance as though transfixed. "There were exactly twenty-five of them, including Rupert. One for every year."

"Were you and Mrs Iverson present?" Clayton asked.

Dennis shook his head. "No, we decided to let the young folk enjoy themselves without us. And now look what's happened!" His forehead was furrowed in anger. "My wife, Suzanna, has MS and is in a wheelchair. She wanted to go, and even ordered a dress. She wouldn't have missed it for the world, but yesterday she had one of her turns so we decided it was best to stay away. I came along simply to welcome the guests . . ." His voice trailed off before he added, "I didn't even say goodbye to Rupert."

"Were any other members of the family at the party?"

Dennis shook his head again, more vigorously.

"No. Our elder son Jeremy wasn't invited. Rupert and he were not close. He stayed with Suzanna to keep her company. And our daughter Heather, the middle one, lives up in Northumberland, so I imagine she thought it was too far to travel, I don't know."

"Any particular reason the two boys weren't close?" Julie asked.

It clearly wasn't the first time Dennis had been asked the question, or maybe he'd mulled it over in the past. He replied straightaway. "We think it went back to when they were young. Jeremy must have been jealous of Rupert, who needed a lot of attention as a baby when his elder brother was already ten. And then later, Rupert went to university whereas Jeremy did an apprenticeship after school. They just took separate paths, that's all."

"We'll need his details," she said. Dennis nodded. "And his sister's. Is she married?"

"Yes, to a GP in Hexham. That's Heather. Her married name is Sanders."

Julie made a note. "Was Rupert a popular person?"

"Oh yes. He wouldn't hurt a fly. Look at how many friends were here last night," said Dennis. "He's an extrovert. I mean, *was*. You'd have to be an extrovert, wouldn't you, to dress up as the Sun King?" His eyes moistened again.

"Has he lived here long?"

"He grew up in this house. Then about three years ago he came back to Tideburgh after dropping out of architectural college in London, though my wife and I had already moved to Norwich by then. I'm paying his rent at a place down the road. He couldn't stay here, obviously, as it's too big for one or two people. And in any case we're renting out the house for parties. We can't sell it because of the coastal erosion." He pointed towards the window facing the sea. Julie got up and looked out. Beyond the flowerbeds in a side garden was the garden wall. On the other side of the wall was a fenced paddock, and only some fifty yards after that, the cliff edge. "It's a big problem, as you probably know, not only for us but for quite a few others in the village. The whole coast is eroding, but this particular area around Happisburgh is the worst affected in the whole of the UK."

"Really?" said Clayton.

Dennis stood up. "Anyway, look, I'd better get back to Suzanna. She's inconsolable."

A techie in white overalls passed the door carrying a camera, which seemed to remind Clayton of something. "Do you have CCTV here, Mr Iverson?"

Dennis shook his head. "We have it, but frankly it's more trouble than it's worth. I've not had it on for a few months."

He took his wallet out of a trouser pocket and produced a business card. "Please get in touch if you need anything." He handed it to Clayton.

They shook hands. Clayton accompanied him to the front door and returned moments later.

"He's not short of a bob or two," he said to Julie. "He arrived in a Rolls."

Julie was still sitting in the armchair where he'd left her. She was staring into space.

"It shouldn't happen like this. Children dying before their parents." The words tumbled out before she could stop herself. She'd evoked her own personal tragedy, the cot death of her first child. There it was, still present in her mind after all these years. She could tell from Clayton's pained look that he'd made the same connection.

"Reet, well," he said briskly. Julie knew that emotions were a foreign country for Clayton, who'd inexplicably take out his own frustrations on an innocent wastepaper basket in the office, to his colleagues' amusement.

She changed the subject. "What did the paramedics say?"

"There's a bash on Rupert's head which raises questions about whether the actual cause of death was drowning. He was face down in the pool. And there are signs of a struggle in the summer house. I've already rung the boss to confirm it's a suspicious death. The SOCOs are checking that there wasn't a break-in."

"Maybe you could give me the grand tour?" Julie said.

"Sure," said Clayton. "Come this way. Let's start with the dining room along here."

He led her past the central staircase into a grand wood-panelled room dwarfed by two long tables where chairs were drawn up for the guests. The settings had been cleared of everything except place mats. But wine glasses and empty bottles were still strewn around the room. Julie resisted the temptation to open a window to let in some fresh air.

"The caterers prepared a banquet for them. The crime scene manager told me they cleaned up the kitchen and took away most of their stuff when they finished last night. But they left glasses with drinks and snacks for the guests when they'd finished. That's what they wanted to pick up this morning," said Clayton.

"All those glasses. What a nightmare for the techies."

Clayton surveyed the detritus. "This party must have cost a fortune."

It took the two of them at least half an hour to explore every room, while forensics dusted for prints and put items into evidence bags. The master bedroom overlooked the swimming pool in the direction of the sea.

"This is where Rupert and Cathy slept. She said they crashed out on the bed at about two in the morning, without taking their clothes off."

They went into two other bedrooms in that wing. One of the beds was made up, spare blankets folded neatly at the end. The other room seemed not to have been occupied.

"Cathy said two other couples stayed the night. But she didn't say which bedrooms they had," Julie said.

"Could be on the other side." Clayton led her back to the staircase and pointed upstairs. "They've got a gym, a sauna and a billiards room up there."

The door to the games room was open. But a scene of chaos awaited them. Cue sticks were on the floor, and wine glasses had spilled their contents onto the table, staining the felt. Half-empty bottles of wine had been left in the corner.

"Pity about the CCTV," Julie remarked.

"What went on here, I wonder?" Clayton pointed to some laughing-gas canisters on a rug.

They went back down to the first floor and into the other wing, where two bedrooms faced onto the front driveway. In one, the duvet was crumpled on top of the bed, and in the other it was flung onto the floor where empty beer bottles were scattered. The place could do with a good airing, Julie thought.

"This must have been some party," she said.

"Did they have orgies at the court of the Sun King?"

"Your guess is as good as mine. The history of Louis XIV is now on my reading list."

"Was he murdered?"

"Who, Louis XIV?" asked Julie. "I've no idea. Why?"

"I'm just thinking, what if one of the guests was role-playing at the party?"

"They were certainly all dressed to kill," Julie commented.

They went downstairs to the kitchen, where everything seemed to be clean and tidy, unlike the other rooms.

"Let's take a closer look at the pool." Clayton headed for the back door.

Julie followed him across a spacious terrace and down some stone steps past a rockery to the poolside summer house. It wasn't the usual kind of old-fashioned structure used for storing poolside furniture, but a sleek modern lounge with a low roof and half-opened bifold glass doors. It was larger than Julie's living room.

Inside, wicker chairs and folding recliners had been pushed aside amid a stack of brightly coloured cushions. Towels had been pulled from shelves and laid on the floor. Empty wine bottles rolled on their sides, waiting to be collected, labelled and analysed.

Julie looked at Clayton. "This place saw some action too last night," he commented.

They turned to face the long pool. Sunlight glinted on the surface. A couple of plastic sun loungers sat side by side at the deep end. On any other day they could have been occupied by sun worshippers relaxing in the late summer warmth.

The techies had marked the spot beside the pool where the body had been recovered from the shallow end. A woman in a white forensics suit was taking samples from the pink-tinged water. It was the only sign that something out of the ordinary had taken place.

"The CSM said they were worried about trace evidence being shed, or even contaminated," Clayton said. "So they took off his clothes before they put him in a body bag."

Julie was relieved that the corpse had been removed. She stood on tiptoes to peer over the wall where the meadow stretched towards the sea.

Clayton turned round, looking back towards the house. "If you were in one of those upstairs rooms, you might not hear anything going on here from this distance, unless there was screaming and shouting."

"Look at that." Julie pointed at a police cordon which ran round the rim of the pasture to a wooden gate at the bottom of the garden. "They've cordoned off the whole boundary. It's going to take ages for them to process their samples."

"So you can get into the garden from there," Clayton said. "Let's go out back and have a look, without disturbing anything."

Julie knew they were both thinking the same thing: that if Rupert Iverson wasn't killed by a partygoer he could have been murdered by an intruder. And if a stranger was suspected, the investigation would ripple out like waves from the body dropped in the pool.

CHAPTER THREE

They retraced their steps through the house and turned to face the entrance.

"It's magnificent, isn't it?" said Julie.

They walked down the drive under the trees, then followed a lane which seemed to lead straight towards the sea. They passed a couple of flintstone cottages where pink hollyhocks bloomed outside the low windows. A little sign announced that one was available for holiday rental. A bicycle was propped up beside the other. The lane became a track, but it stopped abruptly after about two hundred yards in a sudden sheer drop.

"Oh my God," said Julie. "There's no warning or anything." There was only a wooden signpost pointing to the coastal path, which ran perilously close to the edge. At one point, a large chunk was missing. She advanced cautiously and looked down to the sandy beach.

"That must be a fifty-foot drop!" she exclaimed. The jagged edges of the clifftop suggested a fresh fall. She stepped back. "This gives me the willies. I could see the effects of the tidal erosion that Iverson was talking about just from looking through the windows of his house."

She turned to face the direction of Happisburgh where the lighthouse was clearly visible. "In fact, do you remember, a few years ago in Happisburgh there were villagers who refused to move out of their homes until the waves were practically lapping round their feet? Didn't you hear about that?"

"I can't say I remember." Clayton shrugged. "I was still up north, probably. Come on, Julie, let's go round the back of Iverson's place."

They took the coastal path to the paddock that Julie had seen from the house. The path ran alongside the field's wooden boundary fence, which was now sealed off by police tape. A couple of locals were standing at the far end, gesturing towards the house. This would soon be big news in the village, thought Julie.

The two detectives leaned on the fence for a moment. It was a still day, and Julie was enjoying the warm sunshine on her cheeks. Beyond the paddock, she could see a clump of cliffside houses. On a day like this it was hard to imagine the vengeful North Sea tidal surge in full fury destroying cliffs, houses and livelihoods. "I wonder how many of those will be left by the summer holidays next year?" she said to Clayton.

He pointed across the field towards the mansion. "There's the back gate."

They made their way along the path towards Iverson Hall.

"Luckily it was damp last night," Julie said. "Forensics might be able to get some footprints."

"You see the middle of the field there? The grass has been trampled. Maybe the party guests were out here too."

They'd reached the back gate of the property where a sign on the wooden gate announced to visitors: *Private land. Trespassers will be prosecuted. CCTV in operation.*

"Except we know it's not," said Julie.

"Yes, and I wonder who else knows that?" Clayton frowned. "It's padlocked," he went on. "But if you want to get into the house that way, it'd be no trouble. That's where the techies might find something. Fingers crossed, anyway."

He stretched and checked his watch. "Come on, Julie, let's get back. We'll see what Fifi makes of this." Dr Fiona Blackhurst was the dour Home Office chief pathologist, who had no idea of her playful nickname.

They set off to return to the car. "Did you think it strange that Dennis Iverson volunteered that Rupert wouldn't hurt a fly, when I asked if he was popular? I mean, it's a bit of a non sequitur," she said.

"Hmm. Oh yes. There might be something in that." Clayton was still clearly turning over what they'd seen. "Maybe the villagers were jealous of the family with the big house. That's often the way, isn't it? Particularly if he's showing off with his Rolls."

Julie realised she was looking forward to revisiting her childhood memories from this part of the coast in the course of the investigation. But as Clayton opened the car doors, she remembered something.

"Damn."

"What is it?" Clayton asked. He sounded irritated.

"I forgot to ask Iverson about the ghost."

CHAPTER FOUR

They drove off, causing a flare of dust to lift behind them as they turned out of the manor drive.

Julie took out her phone. After a while she turned to Clayton. "I've got news for you. He wasn't murdered. Louis XIV. So much for your theory."

"Oh. What happened to him?"

"He had gangrene. Yuck."

Clayton pulled a face.

"He also had loads of mistresses," she said. "These days, you'd say he was a sex addict."

"Are you suggesting that Rupert . . . ?"

"Just saying."

Just as Clayton was accelerating out of the village, he slammed on the brakes. A combine harvester was trundling along, its width taking up the whole road. He swore under his breath.

"Well, it is harvest time, and they don't work office hours. Just like us." Julie could see bales of straw piled up in the far corner of a field.

"I wonder if Rupert's house is down here. Is this Vicarage Road?" she asked. Clayton nodded, after glancing at the GPS map.

"That's where they live," she said. "He and Cathy have a smallholding somewhere along here."

"Of course they do. They're hipsters, aren't they? We've got to get back."

The combine harvester turned into a farm. They drove on past beet fields in silence for a while, each lost in thought.

"I can just imagine the headlines once the press gets hold of this: 'Louis XIV found dead in Tideburgh swimming pool'," Clayton said after a while.

"After fancy-dress orgy," Julie added. "It's got everything, this murder."

"Let's not get ahead of ourselves." Clayton was grinning.

"Anyway, I'm getting the details of the friends who stayed the night, I guess we should start there," said Julie. "And make some enquiries among the neighbours too."

"Sure," he replied. "Dennis Iverson is going to give us the full guest list. But let's see where we're going with forensics and the post-mortem first."

* * *

Julie caught sight of DCI Bligh watching them from her office window when they pulled into the car park at Anglian Constabulary HQ in Wymondham.

"Don't look up but the boss is waiting for us," she said to Clayton.

He ignored her instruction and squinted towards the corner office on the third floor. "I don't think she was expecting a suspected murder in Tideburgh just after she got back from her summer holiday. Let's take the Tardis up to see her."

All the staff mocked their futuristic HQ, which had been plonked down in the middle of a cornfield outside Wymondham. Colleagues who'd known the old building in central Norwich complained that their splendid isolation hampered their police work, not to mention their social life and pints down the pub. These days a trail of them could be seen popping out at lunchtime to Waitrose or Lidl for a change from the canteen fare.

In the summer months, Julie had taken to driving to Wymondham Abbey with her sandwiches to snatch a few minutes of quiet in the graveyard. It was so peaceful there among the tall pine trees. She'd never yet seen a fellow officer there.

The smell of cooked breakfast wafted into reception as they passed the entrance to the cafeteria. Julie caught Clayton looking wistfully in that direction; it was time for his daily bacon sandwich. He sighed in mock disappointment as he pressed the lift button.

Bligh's office door was ajar and she waved them in. She was a short woman with short hair and a temper to match.

"What's this about Louis XIV in the swimming pool?" was her first question. "Tideburgh isn't exactly Versailles, is it?"

"They call it Tid-bruh, apparently, ma'am," said Clayton. Julie kept her face straight. "Actually, it turns out the party theme was 'the court of the Sun King' because they'd watched *Versailles* on Netflix."

Bligh raised a finely defined eyebrow. "A documentary?" she asked.

"No, no, a historical drama series," Julie explained. "Sex and wigs."

"I see," said Bligh, in a mock reproachful voice. Julie felt awkward, but the others laughed and she joined in.

Bligh motioned to the two chairs in front of her desk and they sat down. Julie had noticed that she didn't keep visitors standing up, probably because they towered over her. Clayton briefed her.

"Bottom line is we can't assume it was one of Rupert's friends from the party," he concluded. "There's access to the grounds via a wooden gate at the back, as well as the main entrance. It would be dead easy to climb over the back gate."

"I see," Bligh said again in her clipped way. "And there's the crucial question of why Rupert left the bedroom. Did he hear something or someone? Or did he go outside to meet someone?"

As usual, Bligh was asking the questions to which they had no answer. Julie and Clayton exchanged a glance.

"Well, ma'am, that's what we need to find out," said Clayton. "And was it an intruder, or someone he trusted?"

Bligh nodded.

Julie and Clayton stood up. "Did you have a good holiday, ma'am?" Clayton asked.

"Excellent, thanks," she replied. "I was hiking up your way, actually."

"Really, whereabouts?" he asked.

"The Yorkshire Dales."

Clayton frowned and cleared his throat. "But I'm from Lancashire."

Julie wondered if Bligh was teasing him. Clayton didn't like to be teased about some subjects.

"Oh yes, so you are. Well, enjoy the rest of your Sunday, both of you."

CHAPTER FIVE

It was late the next afternoon when Julie went over to Clayton's workstation in the detective suite and found him staring out of the window.

"Something up?" she asked him.

He seemed startled by her question. "No, nothing . . . What've you got, Julie?"

She held up a printed sheet of paper. "Details for the people who stayed the night at the manor. I've emailed it to you. I was wondering what you want to do about the Iversons. And Cathy. Not to mention the other guests. But we don't have the full list yet from the father."

"Is it two couples?"

"Yes. The straight couple live together, not far from me in Cossey. The other two, a gay couple according to Cathy, have separate flats in Norwich. One lives in Tombland and the other by the river."

"Reet. But maybe you and I should go and see the Iversons. Why don't you share out the others with Bullard?"

"OK, guv." She checked the time.

"Can you not do it today?" asked Clayton.

"Yes, I can. But Ollie's started a new school this week, and I don't want to get home too late."

"So how old is he now?"

"Eleven. He walks to school on his own now," she said. "Anyway, I was just thinking maybe I should go and see the party guests who live near me, on my way home. And I'll arrange for us to go to see Dennis and Suzanna Iverson tomorrow morning."

"Fine by me. Bullard can interview the other two."

"Sounds like they may be a handful, from what I heard."

* * *

By the time Julie got home that evening, Ollie had retreated as usual to his bedroom.

She found him seated at his desk with his headphones on, playing on his Xbox. So far, so normal.

"Everything go all right today at school?" She had to shout to get his attention. He turned round and nodded, pointed at his headphones, and went back to his game.

She went downstairs to prepare a meal, as it was getting late for Ollie. She thought back to her conversation with the Monahans, on her way home from the nick, which had thrown up some tantalising clues about the Iverson family.

Terry Monahan had come in from work after Julie had already spent half an hour with his wife, Karen, on the patio of their comfortable modern home in the Norwich suburb of Costessey, known locally as Cossey. The flowerbeds bordering the long garden were a riot of colour.

"Sorry I'm late." Terry gave his wife a kiss on the cheek. "It's murder, right?" he asked Julie straight off the bat. He was a partner at a solicitor's firm in the city. Karen had told Julie that she was a maths teacher at a local academy.

"Suspected murder, yes," said Julie. "But we're waiting for more from forensics before we can say that for sure."

Terry shook his head in disbelief. "Dennis Iverson thought that the sun shone out of his arse." Karen pressed his arm and shot an apologetic look at Julie. But he continued:

"Now, if it had been Rupert's dad who'd been murdered, there'd be plenty of suspects, don't you think, darling?"

Julie paused in her note-taking. "Why do you say that?"

"Well, because of how he behaves — he's a bit of a bully, I suppose, likes things to go his way. I guess when you're the boss of a company, you're bound to step on a few toes. He seems to rub some of the locals up the wrong way."

"Oh, I see. But you're not thinking of anything in particular?"

"We don't know the family that well, to be honest," Karen said. "Terry and Rupert were at school together. I only met him a couple of years ago when he came back from London to live in Tideburgh."

Julie turned to Terry. "Was it a local school?"

"You could say that. We were at Wymondham College, but they take in boarders from all over the world, so even though it's the local state school it doesn't really feel like it. Rupert and I became friends on the cricket pitch. Damned good spin bowler. In fact, a group of us played in the field outside the house on Saturday afternoon. That was good fun. A couple of our friends played in their costumes." He smiled at the memory. "Some of the villagers watched from the path behind the fence. We had to ask them to throw back the ball once after it went over the boundary. They refused, though."

"So tell me about this game," said Julie. She wondered how forensics would be able to separate the DNA of a crowd of people who'd trampled all over the grass. "How many of you, for example?"

"There were eight or nine of us. The two of us, Brian and Jonathan — Brian was already in his costume and he did a whole comedy routine, hitching up his skirts to run — and Rupert and Cathy, of course, so that makes six," he said. "Cathy was the umpire. Darling, who were the other two?"

Karen picked up her phone. "I took some pictures, actually. I was fielding, mostly — I know Brian was playing for laughs, but later on when I had my own costume on I rather admired him for playing in that get-up. It was hard to move in those heavy skirts and corsets. Not to mention that bloody wig. And I wore a rather cool gold mask as well. Here we are — Rupert introduced the two others as Max and Adam. Look, that one's got his breeches on. I think he's Adam. The other one with the red hair, with his hands on his hips, that must be Max."

She handed the phone to Julie, who studied the photo. Beyond the small group of cricket players she could make out five or six onlookers on the path — presumably locals or passers-by out for a walk rather than partygoers.

Julie dug into her jacket pocket before offering her business card. "Can you send this photo to me, please? These are my contact details. Did any of the villagers join in?"

A glance passed between the couple.

"No," said Terry. "As I understand it there's a bit of a feud going on between Iverson senior and the villagers, mainly to do with the terrible coastal erosion there. A couple of them have been told their houses are at risk from falling off the cliff but are refusing to move. And also I hear they're not happy about Iverson Hall being a party house — they complain about the guests being too rowdy and stuff like that."

"Excuse me, but what have the other houses in danger got to do with Mr Iverson?"

"He's the chairman of the coastal management team on the district council. I don't know the ins and outs of it as we're not local, but apparently that's why he's not all that popular round there."

"Do you know if any of the villagers were invited to the party?".

Karen laughed. She had a tinkling, infectious laugh. "What do you think? Of course not."

Terry added, "They didn't even clap or anything when Brian was bowled out by Rupert. I thought that was a bit of a strange reaction, to be honest."

The rules of cricket were as foreign to Julie as the court of Louis XIV. She turned to Terry. "Was there any drinking at this cricket match?".

"A bit, yes. Not tea, mainly beers. And nobody brought out cucumber sandwiches," he replied. "Like I say, it was only a bit of fun. We finished up about six and went back to the house to change."

"Where did you put all the kit?" Julie asked.

"You mean the bats and wickets? We dropped them off in the summer house on the way in."

"And at the party itself, did you notice anything in particular that might shed light on this case?" she asked.

"Honestly?" said Karen. "Nothing. It was a great night — everything was laid on and the food was fantastic. I didn't notice anything out of the ordinary. Obviously people were in high spirits, but then it was a party, wasn't it?" Her face clouded over as she remembered how the festivities had ended.

"Did you hear any noises in the middle of the night? You might have heard Rupert walking around?"

Terry replied. "Our bedroom was in a different wing, I think. I don't know for sure. But I slept like a log. We both had plenty to eat and more than a little to drink."

"I thought that your guest room was next to the master bedroom." Julie drew a diagram in her notebook before pointing at the two rooms. Terry and Karen agreed that they'd slept in the same wing as Cathy and Rupert.

"You're right, of course," said Terry. "It's such a big place, I didn't even realise they were there. "

"It seems that more bedrooms were used than there were overnight guests," said Julie.

Terry laughed. "Now there's a surprise."

"What do you mean?"

"Well, it was a party of twenty-somethings . . . what do you expect?"

"So you might be able to explain to me what went on in the billiards room, then?"

Terry frowned. "Is that on the top floor? We had a look round before dinner but didn't go up afterwards, did we, sweetie?"

Karen nodded in agreement. Her hands fluttered around when she spoke, the fingers weighed down by rings. "We stayed in the drawing room where we were trying to dance the minuet with some of the others. They had harpsichord music on a playlist. We were all a bit tipsy, though."

Julie focused back on Karen. "And what about you? Did you hear anything suspicious after you went to bed?"

"Absolutely not, sorry. First thing I heard was Cathy calling up to see what we wanted for breakfast."

"Who did you go as?" Julie asked.

"Terry went as the Duc de Saint-Simon, and I was Louise de La Vallière."

"Who was she? Sorry, I'm not up to speed yet with Louis XIV and his consorts."

"Oh, I'd never heard of her either." Karen laughed again. "She was one of the king's mistresses, his first official one, actually. It was fun doing all the research on our characters. Mine had one leg shorter than the other, so I pretended to limp. I found out that she was brought in as a kind of decoy because there were rumours about Louis XIV and his sister-in-law, Henriette. Well, really her name was Henrietta. She was English, the daughter of Charles I — but she was raised in France from the age of two. You know, after her dad . . ." Karen mimed a guillotine.

"So who went as Henriette?" asked Julie. This party was like speed-dating a history book.

"No idea." Terry was shaking his head too. "All those French names did my head in, frankly," he said.

"Why don't you ask Cathy? Or maybe the hire shop. We got the costumes from a fancy-dress shop in Norwich and they were a great help. I think we all went to the same place," said Karen.

"And that was . . . ?"

"It's a place near the cathedral. I think it's called 'Anything You Fancy'. God, the one who really went to town was Brian. He was in drag as the king's brother, the one who married Henriette." That laugh again.

"He's the one who wore his costume for the cricket match, right?" Julie asked. The two nodded. She glanced at the time. All the talk about royal mistresses had revived her suspicions about Rupert's fidelity, but she had to get home to Ollie.

"Excuse me for asking this, but do you know whether Rupert had multiple sexual partners? I'm wondering whether there was a more personal reason for choosing that theme for his birthday party."

A palpable chill descended. Karen looked across at Terry, who crossed and uncrossed his legs. Nothing was said, then Terry shrugged. *Does he know something?*

Julie leaned forward. "Terry, I'm not quite sure what you mean. Are you saying that Rupert had only one partner, and that's Cathy?"

Terry had recovered his composure. "As far as I know, yes."

CHAPTER SIX

DCI Bligh had called Clayton's major investigation team into the incident room for the first time since Rupert Iverson's death.

Clayton had been invited to the post-mortem that morning with Bligh, who was the senior investigating officer on the case. Julie was not unhappy to have missed it but felt guilty too. As Clayton slid into a seat beside her, Bligh walked to the front of the room. The assembled officers fell silent in expectation.

"Dr Blackhurst has now conducted the post-mortem on Rupert Iverson. The cause of death was drowning, which appears to have been subsequent to a single blow to the head from a blunt object which fractured his skull," she said. "My understanding is that Rupert was still alive when he went into the pool. However there is some bruising around the neck, and throat swelling. The damage to the lungs is such that, according to Dr Blackhurst, it was tantamount to waterboarding."

Julie glanced at Clayton and raised an eyebrow. Waterboarding!

"As for the object with which the victim was attacked, we believe it could be a cricket bat. Thanks to DS Everett"

— Bligh pointed to the photograph of the match that Julie had retrieved from Karen Monahan's phone, on the investigation board behind her — "we know that two cricket bats were stowed in the summer house on the afternoon of the party. However, only one has been found. It's fair to assume that the missing bat is the one used in the attack."

Bligh looked round the room to make sure everyone was paying attention.

"Dr Blackhurst estimates the time of death to be in the early hours of Sunday. So that would confirm what we have heard about him leaving the bedroom, fully clothed, at around 3 a.m."

Bligh consulted some notes, flicking through her notebook. "In terms of toxicology, there are no indications that the victim had consumed alcohol or drugs. However there were nitrous oxide canisters at the property and traces of cocaine on some surfaces. That's about it for now. Although, as you can imagine, it will take a long time to complete the crime scene analysis because of the large number of people who attended the party and the volume of collected samples. We have thousands of pieces that need to be analysed. But I've asked forensics to prioritise the pool area, the summer house and the billiards room."

She looked at the press officer. "What we can confirm is that we're launching a suspected murder investigation. And you can put it out that we're looking for a missing cricket bat. There's a chance, I suppose, that someone might come forward, unless they are deliberately concealing it. I don't need to tell you that we have to get hold of it as soon as possible, for DNA purposes."

The press officer wrote something in her notebook and murmured, "Yes, ma'am."

"Now, about the suspects," Bligh went on. "According to forensics there are no signs of a break-in. So first we need to focus on the twenty-four guests. We need to know why somebody wanted Rupert dead. We shouldn't jump to conclusions here, but let's find out if he had more than one sexual partner. I expect all the guests to have been interviewed over the next few days. Isn't that correct, DI Clayton?"

"Yes, ma'am. We've begun interviewing the guests who stayed the night. And we're talking to the family. The elder brother's coming in, and we're seeing the parents this afternoon."

"Right. Well, let's bear in mind that young men are more likely to be killed by a friend or acquaintance, or even a stranger, but that's no reason to ignore the family connection," said Bligh. "In my opinion, most probably it's an inside job, a guest who saw the opportunity to kill, and who possibly concealed himself after everyone left, then struck."

She paused, as though having an imaginary conversation with herself, weighing the options. After a few more moments, she added, "It's also possible, of course, that the attacker managed to lure Rupert outside. So it may be a gatecrasher in a costume and mask, or someone who gained entrance to the property via the gate into the back garden."

She fixed Clayton with her cold stare. "We should also step up interviews with neighbours and try to get a handle on Rupert's relationships."

"We're talking about a single attacker, but it could have been more than one person," Clayton pointed out. "It could have taken more than one person to hold him down in the pool."

"Exactly. Thank you, DI Clayton. Anything else?" Bligh closed her notebook.

There was a scraping of chairs as they all stood up.

"Waterboarding," Julie said to Clayton as they headed for the door, "that's a bit unusual, isn't it? I mean, it's what they do to terrorists."

"It might mean that Rupert knew something, or had something, that his attacker wanted. I wonder what that was."

Bullard overheard them. "Could be the attacker, or attackers, were trying to break him rather than kill him?" he suggested.

"Yes. Maybe they didn't intend to murder him, just scare him into spilling the beans," Julie agreed. She noticed that Bullard was limping slightly as they left the incident room.

"What happened to you?" she asked.

"Damned dog," he said. "Brian Mason's pug attacked me. Bit me right on the ankle."

* * *

Jeremy Iverson was seated opposite Clayton and Julie in an interview room, his long legs stretched out under the table. Julie scrutinised his face to see whether he resembled the photo of his younger brother on the incident board. Maybe the long nose? They both had the same rangy look. But where Rupert had the brown eyes and round face of his father, Jeremy had piercing blue eyes and chiselled features.

They took down his details. His address was in Great Massingham, where he'd lived alone since his divorce, eight years earlier. Clayton expressed condolences on the death of his brother.

"Thank you." His tone was sombre. "Terrible."

"Where were you on Saturday night?" Clayton asked.

"I was in Norwich with my mother," he said. "She has MS and wasn't feeling up to going to the party."

"And what time did you leave?"

"I stayed the night, actually."

"What time did you go to bed?"

Jeremy paused to think. "I went up just before Dad came back. After the ten o'clock news, it was. I watched the TV press review in my room before going to sleep. It usually sends me to sleep, as a matter of fact."

Julie smiled. "You weren't invited to the party, correct?"

"That's correct. I wasn't expecting to be."

"So you and your brother weren't close?"

"No. It's not compulsory as far as I'm aware."

"Of course. Is there any particular reason?"

"Not on my side, no. We didn't have anything in common, really. He was ten years younger than me, almost a different generation. We didn't have shared friends, or anything like that."

"When was the last time you saw Rupert?" she asked.

He waved a hand in the air. "Last Christmas, maybe. I might have bumped into him at my parents' house at some point. But we don't have family Christmases, as a rule."

"How well do you know the house, Iverson Hall?" Clayton asked.

Jeremy seemed surprised by the question. "You're aware that it used to be our family home until a few years ago? But I've no reason to go there these days."

"You don't have a key for the property?"

"No. It's rented out as a party house. My father couldn't manage to sell it because of the risk from the coastal erosion."

"So is that why he and Mrs Iverson moved to Norwich?"

"The main reason they moved out was because my mother was diagnosed with multiple sclerosis — she needed somewhere more accessible, closer to the hospital."

"We understand you work for the family firm," said Clayton. "What's your job there?"

"When I joined, it was to do the accounts. And some admin. And contacting clients, that sort of thing; I do a bit of everything really. Although I should point out that I started out doing an apprenticeship in construction. My father decided to step back a bit from the business, so he's given me more responsibility."

"So are you expecting to take over from him at some point?"

"That's the idea, yes," said Jeremy. "You may have noticed that the company is called Iverson and Son."

The two detectives ended the interview and showed him out. They watched him leave through the revolving glass door.

"His alibi stacks up," said Julie. "His dad said he was with his mum on Saturday."

"Reet, well let's see what she's got to say about that. If it's not family, we've got plenty more avenues to explore."

CHAPTER SEVEN

Clayton pulled into a gated property surrounded by mature copper beeches on Newmarket Road in Norwich and got out of the car.

"I could have walked here from my place," he muttered.

"Bit of a difference, though, from your neighbourhood," Julie said with a smile. She rather envied Clayton living in the 'Golden Triangle', inhabited by young professionals and yummy mummies, which was only a stroll away from the city centre. They stared up at the gabled three-storey house.

"He's not done badly, has he?" Clayton eyed a Tesla parked on the gravel.

"I suppose they downsized, though," said Julie. She pointed at the spacious double garage. "Do you think his Rolls is in there?"

Clayton's only response was a wink.

A rosy-cheeked woman in an apron opened the front door. Behind her was an older woman in a wheelchair who Julie guessed was Suzanna Iverson. She presumed the young woman must be a carer.

"I'm sorry, my husband's not back yet," Suzanna called out. "Do you mind waiting? Do come in."

She guided them into a large reception room located in the back, with a view of the garden. A flowerbed studded with dahlias encircled the lawn.

"We'd like to speak to you, actually, Mrs Iverson," said Clayton, before doing the introductions.

The young woman was dispatched to the kitchen and returned a few minutes later with tea and biscuits, which she laid out on a large oak coffee table. Julie and Clayton found armchairs. Some art books and fashion magazines were laid out on the table, and the walls of the room were decorated with blown-up photographs of faraway landscapes. But what caught Julie's attention was a full-length portrait of a stunning blonde in a ballgown, who bore a striking resemblance to the person who sat, diminished, before them.

"How can I help you, officers?" Suzanna Iverson asked. "I'm afraid I'm not quite myself, what with all this happening."

She was gripping a crumpled white hanky between red-painted fingernails. The matching scarlet lipstick only served to highlight her complexion, drained of all colour by grief. Her eyes stared at them from deep sockets.

"We're so sorry for your loss," Julie said.

Suzanna acknowledged the condolences with a slight bow of the head and raised the hanky to dab her high cheekbones. Julie had read that she was a former model. Even in her sixties, she was an attractive woman with the presence of someone used to living in the limelight.

"We understand that Jeremy was with you on Saturday evening?" Clayton began.

"Yes, he was. He stayed the night. But he left first thing on Sunday morning, before we heard from Cathy . . ."

"Do you remember what you did on Saturday night? What time you went to bed, that sort of thing?"

"Oh yes. Jeremy and I had supper together. We had a glass of wine or two and so I suggested he stay the night. Dange — she's my helper, who you just met — she came by as usual at half-past eight and put me to bed. I left Jeremy watching the television in there." She gestured towards the next room.

"We understand from your husband that the two brothers aren't — weren't — close?" said Julie.

Suzanna sighed. "What can I say? We did our best. But it's difficult, isn't it? Jeremy has been an absolute brick since I've been ill. He's very attentive. But it's true that Rupert was always my husband's favourite, and I suppose that his elder brother sensed that. I don't think they've been very much in touch for a long time, particularly after Jeremy got married and had a family."

"We understand Jeremy divorced about eight years ago?" Julie asked.

"Yes," came the reply. "Again that was difficult for us because his ex-wife lives in Cornwall now, so we've hardly seen our two grandchildren since they moved. It's very sad. Anyway, is that enough family psychology for you?" She attempted to brighten up, clenching the hanky in her hand.

Julie asked whether Dange was a live-in carer.

"No, she's here most of the day helping out, but then she goes home and pops in during the evening. She's from Lithuania. She's invaluable."

"I understand you've been informed that we're investigating Rupert's death as a possible murder, in the light of the post-mortem examination." The fingers clutched the hanky more tightly, but Suzanna said nothing.

"So we're wondering who might have wanted him dead, Mrs Iverson," Clayton said. "Did he have enemies?"

Suzanna shook her head vigorously. "No, of course not. You saw how popular he is, he had all of his friends at his party. Who would do such a thing? Pushing him into the swimming pool in the middle of the night — it just seems unreal."

Julie asked, "And what about the villagers? Is there any reason why someone might have targeted him?"

"But what are you insinuating?" Suzanna replied, sitting up even more erect. Her blue eyes darted from Julie to Clayton. "He sold his vegetables to the local people. And he made quite a good living from it. What's wrong with that? Honestly, I don't know what you can be referring to."

They heard the sound of the heavy front door closing and turned round to see Dennis Iverson in the hall.

"Ah, here you are," he said. "Sorry I'm late, darling." He went over to his wife and gave her a kiss on top of her head where her blonde hair was gathered into a loose topknot. Then he dropped his laptop onto a seat and sat heavily on the sofa. Dange appeared from the kitchen and Dennis nodded. A few moments later she brought him a cup of tea.

Dennis seemed to have had all the life pumped out of him. He took out a cigarette and waved it at them. "Don't mind, do you?" He lit up before anyone could answer. "Well, what have you found out about who did this?"

"We're pursuing every line," Clayton responded. "We were just asking Mrs Iverson whether any of the villagers had shown any hostility towards Rupert."

Dennis inhaled his cigarette smoke and sank even more deeply into the sofa, his shoulders hunched. "Not so far as I'm aware. We don't live there anymore. But he certainly never mentioned anything."

"When was the last time you saw him?" Julie asked.

"We both saw him together on Friday, the night before his birthday, didn't we, dear? Then on Saturday I went along to do the meeting and greeting at the party. I'd paid for it, after all."

"Did Rupert seem his usual self on Friday?"

"Absolutely," Suzanna replied. "He stayed for supper with the two of us but left straight afterwards to get back to Cathy. There was nothing wrong whatsoever. On the contrary, he was cheerful, looking forward to the party."

Dennis was shaking his head, immersed in his thoughts. After a moment, he said, his voice trembling, "He meant so much to us. We never expected him to come along, did we darling, ten years after Jeremy was born?"

His wife dabbed her eye with a hanky. Iverson glanced across at her with concern, before adding, "He had his whole life ahead of him. Who could have done this? It doesn't make sense!"

"What about Cathy? Was everything all right between them?" Julie asked.

"I believe so," said Dennis, after a slight pause. "We never had any reason to think otherwise. Of course, she's not Bethany, but these things happen. He went to pieces after they split up. I was trying to help him."

"Bethany and Rupert were together at college," Suzanna explained. "They broke up about three years ago."

"Is that Bethany Price?" Julie asked. "I recognise her name from the party guest list. So what was special about her?"

Suzanna replied. "She sparkled, didn't she, darling?"

Dennis nodded in agreement. "That's exactly it. She made you feel special to be in her company. Although I must say the way she dropped him was rather brutal. We don't know if there was anyone else involved. We didn't dare ask, did we?"

Suzanna didn't reply, no doubt lost in the fog of grief.

"One more thing, Mr Iverson," Clayton asked. "How difficult would it be for a stranger to get into the house? It strikes me that it's pretty easy for a passer-by to hop over the gate into the property."

"You're right, yes. But Tideburgh is such a quiet place, who would do that? And to get into the house, they'd need a key, unless one of the doors had been left open."

Julie dutifully wrote that down and stared at her notebook. She could imagine a party full of young people perhaps enjoying themselves too much to lock the doors, a manor accessible to all from the coastal path . . . The killer could be anyone.

CHAPTER EIGHT

Julie looked up at the sign of Anything You Fancy in Elm Hill. The shop window on the cobbled street, a stone's throw from the spire of Norwich Cathedral, displayed mannequins dressed in Charleston outfits, and advertised 'costumes for every occasion'.

Even death.

She pushed open the door, prompting a tinkling bell to sound. She had entered an Ali Baba's cave filled with frocks of all shapes and sizes, protected by polythene, hanging on rails which filled the store. She could hear the hum of a sewing machine. She waited by the counter until a bald, middle-aged man with glasses pushed up onto his forehead and a tape measure hanging round his neck emerged from the back.

"Morning," he said. "Are you looking for something in particular?"

Julie held up her warrant card. "DS Julie Everett, Anglian Constabulary. We're investigating a suspected murder at a party in Tideburgh at the weekend."

"You mean Iverson Hall? I was expecting a visit." He lowered his glasses onto his nose and inspected the card for a moment before pushing them back up again. " I saw the article in the paper. Very sad."

"I understand most of the costumes were rented from you, Mr . . . ?"

"Underwood. All of them were, I believe. It's not everyone who can deliver two dozen seventeenth-century costumes. I had to get some of them run up here. Luckily we had plenty of notice. That's the thing about birthday parties . . . you can plan in advance."

"Yes. Would you still have the order details?" Julie asked. "We're wondering whether there were exactly twenty-five costumes, which would correspond to the number at the party. You never know, there might be a discrepancy."

"Just a moment." He disappeared behind a curtain. Through the crack, Julie saw two women seated in front of sewing machines. They must be working on another order. She flicked through some of the garments on the rails while she waited. Hats, exotic headwear and feather boas were placed on a table. She couldn't remember the last time she'd been to a fancy-dress party. Not that long ago she'd had to put together a costume for Ollie, who went as a gladiator to a party with some schoolmates. But that hadn't been too taxing a challenge — she'd tacked tea towels together under a belt.

"Here we are," said Underwood, coming back into the store. He placed a file on the counter and flipped it open. "It's Iverson, isn't it?"

Julie nodded and took out her phone. "I'll need a copy of this." Mr Underwood let her photograph two pages and then counted the number of entries.

"That's it," he said. "Twenty-six."

"Twenty-six?" Julie repeated. How could that be? Could the attacker be the person who rented the twenty-sixth costume? And would they be so careless about giving the game away? Then she remembered Suzanna Iverson, who had ordered a costume for herself before deciding not to attend.

"Do you have the real names of all the guests?" She frowned at the list. "You seem to have put down the names of the Versailles courtiers, not the party guests."

"Oh yes, I can get that for you. But I found it easier that way for the invoice. It was a centralised order, you see. Dennis Iverson paid for the whole thing."

"Yes, he mentioned he'd funded the party. I didn't realise he meant the costumes too." She took another look at the invoice. It had been paid in full two weeks before the party. "When did everyone take delivery of the costumes?"

"Oh, most of them came in the week of the party. I was going to take Mrs Iverson's dress round on Saturday, but she told me she was too poorly to go. She'd have looked wonderful as Anne of Austria."

"Do you know who decided who came as which character? Was it a free choice or did Rupert give instructions? I mean, it's possible that he could have had two people coming as the same courtier unless it was properly organised."

"Just a moment." Underwood returned behind the curtain again. He re-emerged with two sheets of handwritten paper.

"It's a bit of a mess, I'm afraid," he said. "You see, Rupert came up with his own list of characters for some of his friends, probably his closest ones, and then I made some suggestions which were added. There was some duplication, which you can see from the crossing out." He held out the papers.

"I'd be interested to see who went as Henrietta," said Julie.

"Ah, yes. The wife of Monsieur." Underwood searched through his pockets, then picked up a sheaf of invoices from the counter and looked underneath then. Finally, he opened a drawer and began riffling through it, becoming increasingly agitated. "Now where did I put my glasses?"

Julie pointed to his head.

"Ah, yes! Thank you." He pulled them down to look through the list. "Henriette, Henriette, let's see." He let out a guffaw. "In the role of Henriette was a Mr James Crofton."

Julie raised an eyebrow. Nobody had mentioned that a second partygoer had been in drag.

"You are aware that the king's brother was a homosexual, Detective Sergeant? He married a woman due to social convention, but it seems nobody at court was duped."

"Yes, of course."

Julie's head was spinning. Who was James Crofton and why had Rupert paired him off with Brian Mason? After all, Brian was in a relationship with Jonathan Murray, who was given the role of his historical character's lover. But why hadn't Rupert made Jonathan Brian's 'wife' at the party?

Could it be a private joke, or something more sinister, she wondered.

"You can have these." Underwood interrupted her train of thought by proffering the notes. "I've no more use for them. But you can see that I'm not only in the rental business, I also have to be an amateur historian, and more."

* * *

Julie grabbed a sandwich from Crocodile near the cathedral and set off for Tideburgh. She'd offered to do more poking around the village while the rest of the team continued to work through the party's guest list.

She was glad to be out of the office, and her spirits lifted after she turned off the main road to drive down hawthorn-lined lanes.

On her way into Tideburgh, she passed a small caravan site close to a pub called the Smugglers Arms. This would be a good place to start. She parked her Clio outside, walked past a couple of empty tables outside the cream painted building and made for the bar. A couple of elderly men were sipping their drinks, talking to the barman. But her attention was drawn by some black-and-white photographs on the wall.

They showed the village in the old days. She leaned forward for a closer look. They mostly depicted the farming community, tilling the fields. But her attention was caught by one in which concrete pillboxes could be seen poking up through the wheat.

Julie turned to the barman. "Do you have a moment?" she said, holding up her warrant card. "You've heard about Rupert Iverson's death?"

"Yes. It's a bad business." He excused himself from the conversation and they moved down to the other end of the bar, out of earshot of the other customers.

"Are you the owner?" Julie asked.

"That's right. Simon Keeble." His shaven head drew attention to his pointy ears, which reminded Julie of Spock in *Star Trek*.

"Is there anything you might have heard about, or noticed, that could shed any light on his death?" she said.

"Not that I can think of. You mean, who would want Rupert dead?"

She nodded.

"Beats me. You know he and his girlfriend have a smallholding in the village?"

"Yes, I'm on my way to see her. And the Iverson family's well known round here, I presume."

"Oh yes. Rupert's parents moved away, of course, a few years ago," said the landlord. "But I can't say that Dennis Iverson is the flavour of the month in Tideburgh."

"What do you mean?"

"You should ask the people who are going to lose their homes. Richard Fairbairn and Iris Haggett, for starters."

Julie jotted down the names and waited for an explanation.

"You see, Dennis Iverson is on the district council, with the portfolio for coastal management. And they blame him for condemning their homes. Even though it's one of the paid officers they're dealing with after their homes were declared unsafe."

"Oh yes, I heard something about that."

"These two are still hanging on. But there's no money to move them to another plot, not like a few years ago in Happisburgh when the government agreed a pilot scheme with the council. Anyway these two are refusing to budge. There've been a few slanging matches at public meetings with council members, if you want to know."

He shook his head. "All it would take would be another storm surge and that'll be it for them. Curtains," he went on. "It's so unstable because the cliffs are soft clay and sand. So that's why those properties on Blackberry Lane are vulnerable. And what really pisses off people is that Dennis Iverson now lives in Norwich and is taking decisions about what happens in Tideburgh."

Julie was struggling to see how this might be connected to Rupert Iverson's death.

"Yes, but Mr Iverson does own a house here," she pointed out.

"And that's another thing. It's a party house, and that's got people complaining. I don't mind too much because a lot of them come in here, but you talk to villagers and they'll say they can't stand these folks from outside coming in, parking their cars all over the place, and making a noise at all times of day and night. God knows what's going on at that house. This is a very family-orientated place, the villagers have young children and people say that Dennis Iverson's to blame for the racket and disruption."

"I imagine the local economy needs the tourists," Julie pointed out. "I mean, I came here on holiday as a youngster."

The landlord was getting into his stride. "That's not what I'm saying. You have to understand how the locals feel," he said, "particularly when you see men dressed up as women prancing around playing cricket outside the house. What the hell is going on?"

Julie stared at him, swallowing a sharp retort. This was prejudice, pure and simple. He must imagine Iverson Hall as a den of iniquity. But there was no point in calling out his homophobia; it wouldn't solve the mystery of Rupert Iverson's death. She put away her notebook. "Are you local yourself, Mr Keeble?"

"Born and bred. My family are originally from Walcott, over the other side of Happisburgh. But I didn't want to be a farmer like my dad and ended up here."

"So maybe you could tell me what those small towers are in the photo?" she asked, pointing to the pub entrance.

"Oh, those are military pillboxes just down the lane." Keeble gestured towards the sea. "If you go to Happisburgh you'll see more of them. It's what's left of a whole network of tunnels they dug during the war. They're under the old gun batteries. We played in the tunnels when we were kids. I dare say some still go down there, although a lot of them have collapsed."

"So they're nothing to do with smuggling, then?" Julie said. "I read that there are rumours about a smuggler's hoard in the manor."

"Oh, that. I wouldn't believe everything you read on the internet. Anyway, they'd have to dig up the house if they went looking for treasure."

"But what about the ghost of Iverson Hall?"

The landlord burst out laughing. He'd recovered his good humour. "Just because it's draughty doesn't mean there's a ghost. It's probably a story Iverson made up to get more bookings for his party house."

He returned to his customers and Julie thanked him as she left. But she was struck by his harsh reaction to the cross-dressing at Rupert's birthday where the guests were just having a bit of fun at a cricket match before his 'sex and wigs' party. How many of the villagers shared the publican's views in this remote part of Norfolk? Clearly prejudice still ran strong around here. But strong enough for murder? Could it be an enraged villager who had climbed over the gate in the middle of the night, somehow lured Rupert outside and bludgeoned him with a cricket bat before shoving him into the pool? The idea seemed ludicrous.

CHAPTER NINE

Julie checked her watch when she left the pub. She still had time to explore before going to see Cathy.

She loved wandering round these pretty villages along the North Norfolk coast, but now her memories were stained by some of the gruesome and horrific murders the team had investigated. She took the car in the direction of the sea and found a lane which petered out beside a recently harvested wheat field, where she parked. On the far side of the field she could see one of the abandoned gun batteries mentioned by Keeble.

It was close to the cliff edge. She skirted round the field and picked up the coastal path in its direction, buffeted by the strengthening wind. At times, she stepped off the path into the field to avoid getting too close to the lip of the cliff where fresh clay under tufts of grass signalled that clods had sheared off onto the beach below. The earth was soft under her feet. *What if it collapses underneath me? What if a gust of wind pushes me off the cliff?*

After less than ten minutes' walk she reached a low concrete shelter and peered inside. Someone had written *Mark loves Kelly* on an upper joist which faced the sea. The unmistakable stench of urine filled her nostrils. *People are still coming here*. She advanced gingerly towards the back, where she saw steps leading down to a dark hole which was partially covered over. It was big enough to still be an entrance to a tunnel below. She almost tripped over some charred wood on the ground. A faint smell of smoke rose from the ash. Someone had built a fire here, maybe the night before.

She retraced her steps, her eyes glued to the path. After a few minutes, she stopped to admire the view, but she didn't want to linger. This place felt sinister. Looking back across the field towards the village, she caught sight of a dilapidated pillbox beside a hedge. It was clear that these concrete buildings must be connected by a tunnel. Tideburgh was beginning to surrender its secrets.

* * *

A few minutes later, Julie drew up in front of a cottage on Vicarage Road. The building had clearly been extended in recent years, the original house being in flintstone with two red-brick extensions on either side.

There was no sign of Cathy when Julie rang the front doorbell, so she walked around the house. In the back she found neat rows of lettuce and potatoes in a sizeable vegetable patch. A little further away she could make out clusters of tomatoes, ripe for the picking, under a plastic dome. Hens were scratching at grain in a large run attached to their coop. Julie could see Cathy's sturdy figure standing in her wellies by the fence at the far edge of the property. She was waving her jacket at a flock of geese.

"Shoo! Fuck off, you lot," she was shouting at them. After a few moments she noticed Julie and came over.

"Did you see them?" she said. "Pink-footed geese. They're feeding on the sugar beet tops in the farm next door. Next thing you know they'll be over here. It happens every year. Bloody annoying. And very noisy as well."

"I'm afraid I've never heard of pink-footed geese," Julie said. "But I know Canada geese are a pest."

"Don't get me started," Cathy snorted. "They're the worst. They poop all over the place. Horrible pests. Anyway, hello."

"Hello," Julie replied. "Do you have a few minutes?"

She picked her way behind Cathy along a muddy path through the vegetable patch. "Nice operation you've got going here," she commented.

"Yes. We've been doing really well. I was about to give up my job at the dairy because this is taking up so much of my time. We were thinking of hiring someone to help out, maybe next season — there are plenty of pickers staying on the caravan site. And Rupert was talking to the farmer next door about selling us the field by the fence."

"And?"

Cathy pulled a face. "He didn't want to sell. It was frustrating. Rupert was very put out. We were talking about moving but that wouldn't have been simple either. But a lot of our outgoings were still being covered by Rupert's dad. I've put my time and money into it, but, well, now I don't know what I'm going to do."

Julie caught a crack in her voice. "Are you OK?" she asked.

Cathy gave a thin smile. "Come in and have some tea."

Julie took off her shoes while Cathy left her boots at the door and hung up her jacket. They sat down at the kitchen table while waiting for the kettle to boil.

"How are you doing, really?" Julie said softly.

"Oh, you know." Cathy kept her eyes on the kettle. "It's tough. People have been very nice." Her face clouded over, and she seemed on the point of tears. She got up and poured two mugs of tea.

Julie took out her notebook.

"Are you getting anywhere?" Cathy asked. "I was called by a journalist from the *EDP* but I didn't want to talk to him. I just said what a lovely person Rupert was and that you're trying to find out how he drowned."

"Yes, I saw that," Julie said. She knew that Clayton was friendly with the crime reporter of the *Eastern Daily Press*,

Luke Martin, whom she occasionally saw at press conferences. She'd long suspected that he was getting confidential information from Clayton, who probably received tip-offs in return.

"What was Rupert really like, Cathy? I mean it was a rather flamboyant way to celebrate a birthday, wasn't it?"

The young woman bristled. "Well, first of all, his dad was paying for it. It was like money was no object. I think that was more down to his dad than to Rupert. Maybe Mr Iverson wanted to show off to the villagers. But I could see that Rupert was thinking about the party when we were watching *Versailles* on TV. He'd already decided he wanted fancy dress, so it seemed pretty obvious, I suppose."

"Did Rupert have a good relationship with his father?"

"Oh, yes. I think his dad was proud of what he was doing here. Mr Iverson was always very encouraging. He had dinner with his parents on the night before the party."

"I see," said Julie. "And how long had you and Rupert been together?"

"Almost two years, it would be. I worked on the dairy farm, you see, and we met when he was looking for help with the smallholding — I can turn my hand to most outdoors work." She paused. "And then, one thing led to another."

Then she blurted out, "I don't think Mr Iverson likes me much."

Julie looked up from her notebook. "Is there anything in particular that makes you think that?"

"No. He never said anything, he was always very polite, but you know, at arm's length. I think he thought I was below Rupert's station. Not worthy, you know?"

"Like a class thing?" Julie asked.

"Yeah. Kind of," said Cathy. "If you know what I mean."

Indeed I do, Julie thought. *I see it every day at the nick.*

"But it pisses me off, because Mr Iverson was a nobody when he started out," Cathy continued. Julie felt sorry for Cathy but could see that this conversation was going nowhere.

"Now, think back to the night of the party," she said, steering the conversation onto more relevant ground. "Do you remember whether your bedroom window was open? And were the curtains drawn in your bedroom that night?"

"As I recall, yes, we did draw the curtains. I'm not sure about the window," Cathy replied. "It was a chilly night, so it was probably closed. It gets cool here by the sea at night. But why do you want to know that?"

"We're trying to find out why Rupert would have left the bedroom when he did. He might have heard something, you see."

"Oh. Right." Cathy took a sip of tea and stared at Julie with green cat's eyes.

"And you never heard a splash in the pool during the night? Or any other noises? A struggle?"

Cathy shook her head firmly.

"I need to double-check which bedrooms were occupied by the two couples who stayed the night. Were they in the same wing as you?"

"Terry and Karen had the room next door to us. And we put Brian and Jonathan in the other wing."

"If I'm not mistaken, it's your bedroom window that overlooked the pool, correct?"

"Yes," Cathy said, warily.

"And what about the other wing? As I recall, those bedrooms don't have a view over the pool."

"No, they don't. They overlook the front drive."

"By the way, Cathy, do you remember who went to the party as Henriette, the wife of the king's brother?"

Cathy looked blank. "No, why? Rupert was the one who decided—"

"Does the name James Crofton ring a bell?"

"You mean it was a guy who went as her?" Her surprise appeared to be genuine. She burst out laughing. "That's a good one! I suppose it could be a friend of Brian."

"And might this be a joke that Rupert was playing on Brian, by marrying him off to another man?"

Cathy frowned. "I think you could be reading too much into this. It was a party, that's all. And anyway, Brian was there with Jonathan."

"Yes, but Rupert was taking the roles extremely seriously. Henriette was the Sun King's mistress, wasn't she? Have you any reason to think that he might have been bisexual?"

"Bisexual? Rupert? Of course not!" Cathy exclaimed. "Anyway, Louis XIV had a lot of mistresses, didn't he, and the others were at the party too, including me as the mistress-in-chief, so are you suggesting Rupert actually slept with all of us?"

Julie wasn't deterred. "Sorry, Cathy, I know this must be tough, but I have to look at this crime from every angle if I'm to find out who killed Rupert." She decided to plunge on. "Did you ever suspect Rupert of being unfaithful?"

Cathy's eyes flew open and she blushed, as though she'd just been caught with her hand in the cookie jar.

"Unfaithful?"

"You mentioned the last time we spoke that you and Rupert had had problems in the past. It would be helpful if you could explain. And frankly, judging by the state of some of the rooms, there was some sexual activity going on during your 'sex and wigs' party."

Cathy thought for a moment before responding. "What's that got to do with what happened to Rupert?"

"I'm not suggesting anything, but there's a possibility that *if* he was sleeping with somebody else and the partner of that person found out, then the partner might be extremely jealous."

"Oh, I see. I hadn't thought of that. You don't mean that I . . . ?"

"No," said Julie. "I'm not suggesting that you killed him." *Could she have?*

"OK, well —" Cathy's words came tumbling out in a rush — "he was seeing his ex-girlfriend, Bethany."

"Did you mention this to him?"

"Yes. *I accused him*, a couple of weeks ago."

"And how did he react?"

"Oh, he denied it. But she was messaging him. I couldn't read them because his phone's always locked, but I could see her name popping up all the time. New message from Bethany, new message from Bethany. Again and again. I think he'd been deceiving me for some time."

She seemed to have forgotten a detective was interviewing her. As though talking to herself, she went on, "I just don't get it. She was the one who broke up with him. I thought he'd moved on." Then she looked straight at Julie. "Yes, would you believe it? After we got together, he'd talk about her — not that I wanted to know anything particularly. He'd get a dreamy look in his eye and say things like, 'Bethany's perfect.' Well, you can imagine how I felt about that, can't you?"

Julie tried to coax Cathy back to the matter in hand. "Did Bethany have a partner? Do you have any reason to suspect that he knew about this?" she asked. "Or anyone else, for that matter."

"I don't know. Sorry. Nobody mentioned it to me, and as for Bethany and Jacob, I don't really know either of them very well. They're not local to Tideburgh, you see."

"But they were at the party?"

"Oh yes. Both of them." Cathy seemed to be on the point of saying more but bit her lip.

"Did you notice any animosity at the party? Any hostility from Bethany's boyfriend, for example?"

Cathy picked up her mug and nursed it. Then she replied, "Bethany was trying to monopolise Rupert's attention. She was very touchy-feely at the party with him. But Jacob was off talking to other people. I can't say he reacted in any particular way. But then, I was trying to make sure that everyone was enjoying themselves, and there were twenty-four other people to take care of."

"Is there anything else, Cathy?" Julie asked. "What happened in the billiards room? It was a mess."

"Oh. I know. I noticed that the next morning when I was looking for Rupert. But I've no idea who was up there on

Saturday night. I couldn't stop Rupert's friends from wandering round and enjoying themselves, could I?"

Cathy continued to stare at Julie as though weighing up what to say. Then she said in a soft voice, "Actually, I was going to end it with Rupert. I found a ginger hair last week under the pillow when I was making the bed. He'd brought her to our house, right here!"

"Did you . . . Wait a minute, didn't you tell me the other day that you'd sorted out your problems?" Julie couldn't hold back a flash of anger. Was Cathy covering something up?

Cathy shook her head. "I kept it to myself — Rupert never found out that I knew. I was going to wait until after the party. I decided it wouldn't be fair, on his birthday . . . but now I wonder what would've happened if I'd said something. Now I feel as though I'm the one being punished because he's gone!"

* * *

Julie got back into the car, drove a short distance and parked on the verge of a field. She felt troubled by the conversation. She rang Clayton, who picked up straight away.

"Got anything, Julie?" he asked. She told him about her conversation with Cathy.

"Well done," said Clayton. "We'll get Bethany and Jacob in ASAP."

"And there's another thing," said Julie. "I know how I can double-check what Cathy said about Rupert's relationship with Bethany."

She was sure that Terry Monahan, Rupert's friend from their school days, would help her with that if she stopped in on the way home, perhaps speak to him without his wife present. Terry struck her as a protective friend who might not want Karen to know Rupert was cheating on Cathy, even now he was dead.

But she was still troubled by the pub landlord's rant about Dennis Iverson and the house. Before setting off again she googled Iverson Hall, which popped up on a rental platform. The house was described in glowing terms as the perfect setting for parties, weddings and receptions: *isolated eight-bedroom manor boasting swimming pool, gym, billiards room and spacious reception rooms*. A couple of comments praised the lovely surroundings and expressed thanks for a wonderful stay. There were no negative comments. But perhaps the site was curated.

The house was also advertised on its own Facebook page. But the comments extolling the 'peaceful' village and 'idyllic setting' were mixed with insulting and homophobic messages that had been liked by dozens of people. One message read, *Not recommended for family groups. This rental is usually a destination for the gay community*. The message had been shared several times. Another comment said, *This party house is great for raves. Throw your inhibitions to the winds! Strongly recommended.* That message had attracted replies, presumably from villagers, instructing the '*fornicating*' visitors to '*take your Chelsea tractors back to Chelsea!*'

The messages had been posted in the previous months. They reflected the resentment the pub landlord had displayed. Could the comments have been posted by Keeble under a different name, or by other villagers, or even by outsiders? Julie couldn't be sure. But the most chilling messages dated from the day after Rupert Iverson's death. One read: *The owner's son has died in mysterious circumstances at a fancy dress orgy at the hall.*

A reply to that message said, *So that's what the owner spends his corrupt earnings on*. It was accompanied by a series of LOL emojis.

CHAPTER TEN

The next morning, Julie was so engrossed reading the record of Bullard's interviews with Brian Mason and Jonathan Murray that she didn't hear her phone ping. She jumped when Clayton approached her workstation.

"Have you seen the *EDP*?" he asked.

"No, why?"

"Take a look."

She went to the *Eastern Daily Press* site where a headline read: *Guests questioned in Iverson family scion death riddle*. Nothing wrong there. But it was the accompanying photograph which caught her attention. It showed Rupert Iverson dressed as Louis XIV standing next to two glamorous women in wigs wearing low-cut dresses with pinched waists. The caption read, *Rupert Iverson at his twenty-fifth birthday party in Tideburgh with two guests*. It was only on closer inspection that Julie could see that one of the women had large and powerful hands.

"Is that Brian Mason next to Rupert? I wonder how the hell they got hold of this photo!"

"Yes. But that's not all. Wait till you see this," said Clayton. "Someone's been doing some digging." He took out his phone and showed her a link to an online gossip site. There, the headline was more explicit: *Gay couple questioned over Iverson*

Hall death. Like the newspaper, the gossip site mentioned that Rupert's guests had attended a party entitled 'In the court of the Sun King'. But the site went on to describe the sexual antics at Versailles and included background on the Norwich gay clubbing scene. The innuendo would have left no doubt in readers' minds about a suspected 'gay killer' among the birthday revellers. The article concluded with a link to the Netflix TV series.

"That's helpful of them," said Julie. She pursed her lips and handed back the phone to Clayton.

He sat down next to her and sighed. "That's what comes up if you google Iverson Hall. But what people don't know is that the sole reason we interviewed those two was because they happened to stay overnight at the house. Thank God they're not named here."

"Bligh needs to stamp on this, doesn't she?" said Julie. "It's so misleading, unless they've got specific information about a so-called gay angle." She made a face. "It's basically a rumour put out there as fact. But it also shows the local interest in this case. Cathy told me yesterday that she'd been contacted by the *EDP*."

"Well, I don't mind journalists doing their job, but we don't want to start any hares running before we've had a chance to get anywhere. I'll deal with Bligh." He stood up to go.

"Anyway, from what I just read on the system, Brian Mason and Jonathan Murray sounded very helpful. But talking about jumping to conclusions, look at this." She called up Iverson Hall's Facebook page.

He leaned over her shoulder to read it on the screen. "Oh, shit, Julie, that's ugly. They've got it in for Dennis Iverson because of what they think goes on at the manor."

"I know. I'm going to call him about it right now."

"Who was it who said something about a lie travelling halfway round the world before the truth can even get its boots on? Isn't that what's going on here?"

"Was it Mark Twain? Let me check," Julie typed the beginning of the quote into Google. They leaned forward to see the answer. "Oh. A misquotation. They don't seem to know where it's come from. Well, we don't know if the orgy reference is a lie or not — but rumours are certainly travelling round Tideburgh."

Clayton stood up. "Did you get the confirmation about Rupert and Bethany having nookie?"

Julie smiled. Clayton always used such quaint expressions. *Must be a northern thing.*

"Yes I did. I called in on the Monahans. You know, the other two guests who stayed the night?"

He was nodding vigorously, as if to say, *Get to the point.*

"Terry Monahan seemed to know more than he said when I saw them the other night. I'd asked them about whether Rupert had other sexual partners. Anyway, yesterday, when I told him about Cathy's suspicions, he confirmed that Rupert and Bethany had rekindled their relationship a couple of months ago."

"Why did he lie the first time you asked him?"

"He was a bit embarrassed to talk about it in front of his wife, it seems — probably didn't want her thinking badly of Rupert or Bethany. But according to him, Rupert was going to ditch Cathy for Bethany."

"Oh. He was one of Rupert's school friends, right?"

"That's right. So he'd obviously confided in him. Terry seems to know more about the relationship than Cathy did, in fact. Ironically, Cathy told me that she was going to finish with Rupert after the party."

"Thanks, Julie. I want Kev to do Rupert's phone before we speak to Bethany," Clayton said. Kevin Fuller was the IT chief who knew every data-extraction trick in the book.

"Their generation is supposed to do everything online, aren't they?" he added.

"Yes," Julie replied. "That might be true for Rupert and his millennial friends, but we don't know that the attacker is one of them."

Clayton was about to head in the direction of the cafeteria but she stopped him. She held up the papers she'd brought from the costume rental boutique.

"And guess what, guv?" she said. "Bethany went to the party as Madame de Maintenon."

He looked blank.

"She was Louis XIV's secret wife. I checked."

"So this guest list is like a kind of code? And Rupert held the key by deciding who went dressed as who?"

"Looks like it," said Julie. "It must have amused him. The guests might have researched their own character, but not necessarily all the others. It's not as though everyone knows the history of Louis XIV or watched *Versailles*."

"What a devious bastard."

"That's not all." She told him that James Crofton had attended the party as the king's sister-in-law.

"So that's two of them who were at the party in drag? And who's this sister-in-law?"

"Henriette. She was married to Monsieur, the king's brother who was basically homosexual."

"You mean the prince was actually a queen?"

"Is that supposed to be a joke?" said Julie, sternly. "Brian Mason was at the party in the role of Monsieur, who often dressed in women's clothes, by the way — that's why he went in a frock. You may recall that he was in costume for the cricket match on the afternoon of the party. The landlord of the pub in Tideburgh was quite het up about that."

"Judging from the picture in the paper, Brian Mason's obviously quite a character," said Clayton with a smile. "I wish we'd known all this when Bullard interviewed him. He'll have to go back to Brian Mason. He said he was very upset about Rupert."

"The point is, we need to know if there was a particular reason why James went dressed as Henriette. It just so happens that Henriette also became the king's mistress before she came to a sticky end. So, as Rupert was Louis XIV, it could point to a relationship between him and James Crofton. Or at least between Crofton and Brian Mason. Are you still with me?"

"It sounds a little convoluted. But from what you're saying there could be a gay angle to the murder after all? I mean, with Rupert deciding to give a guy the role of the king's mistress. Or let's face it, it could also be just a fancy-dress party with a special theme." He took the list from Julie and began to study it. "Though these crossings-out could be precious in terms of how he saw his friends."

Julie nodded. "Exactly. Rupert was the puppet master. But I need more time to figure out who was who in the court. Maybe we should catch up on the TV bonkathon as well. But we have to go where the evidence takes us, don't we, not nasty insinuations from a gossip site. And these guys were Rupert's friends. Why would any of them want to kill him?"

He put down the papers with a flourish. She didn't even know if Clayton had a TV. He spent his free time playing classical guitar, from what she knew.

"There's one other thing, guv, from yesterday," she went on. "I can't decide whether it's important though."

He began drumming his pen on her desk.

"Shoot."

"Well, it could be significant that Dennis Iverson is the chairman of the local council's coastal management team. And as such, he has direct responsibility for the plight of the villagers whose homes are threatened by the sea."

"And how many are affected by that?" Clayton asked.

"Well, the pub owner gave me the names of two property owners on Blackberry Lane, but they're the ones closest to the sea. He said their homes have been declared unsafe but so far they're staying put. I think that others on the lane may also be at risk. But I'm not sure whether it's relevant to our investigation into who killed Rupert."

"Let's park that idea for now. I reckon that the theory about Bethany and Rupert and the green-eyed monster looks like a much more promising line of enquiry. A crime of passion." Clayton wrinkled his nose and pursed his mouth. "Still, everything keeps coming back to Dennis Iverson, doesn't it?"

CHAPTER ELEVEN

Julie printed out the social media posts before picking up the phone. She reached Dennis Iverson in his Norwich office.

"Have you arrested someone already?" he asked in a guarded tone. "I see that you've been interviewing the party guests. I was not at all happy to see a photograph of Rupert from the party without having been informed about it. It gave Suzanna a terrible shock."

"I'm sorry to hear that, Mr Iverson," said Julie. "We didn't release the photo to the press."

A sound that sounded like a harrumph came down the line. Julie then asked how regularly he checked the Facebook page of Iverson Hall.

"Not often, why?" he replied.

"I'd suggest that you take a look at the comments right now, particularly the one that dates from just after Rupert died," she said. There was a silence in which Julie imagined him calling up the website and scrolling down. Then came an explosion.

"But this is outrageous!" he exclaimed. "What's all this about orgies? It's libel! I'm going to delete these comments immediately and report this outrage to Facebook!"

"Have you any idea who might have written them? Do you recognise any names?"

"Of course not. They must be fake identities. This is fake news!" he shouted. Julie heard him put down the phone before shutting the door noisily. She could picture him, his face reddened with rage, returning to his desk before taking out a cigarette. Sure enough, there was the click of a lighter, followed by a loud exhalation.

"Mr Iverson, you can file a complaint to the police if you wish," Julie said.

That produced a further explosion. "But you're the police!" he shouted. "And so far you haven't produced a single suspect in the murder of my son!"

Julie tried another tack. "Could I just ask you about the other post, which seems to suggest that some locals object to Iverson Hall being rented out to, as they put it 'the gay community'?"

Dennis spluttered, "Rented out to the gay community? What on earth are they talking about? Honestly, in all the years that we've been renting out the house, maybe there's been one gay club night held there. And the only reason I know is because some in the village complained. Honestly, who fucking cares?"

Julie held the phone away from her ear and turned to see whether any of her colleagues could hear the expletives coming down the line, but everyone had their backs hunched in concentration over their computers.

"Well, Mr Iverson, it's another angle for us to look at, see if we can find a motive for an attack on Rupert — outraged neighbours, for example."

"What on earth do you mean? Who's been complaining now?"

"I heard that some of the villagers took offence at one of Rupert's friends playing cricket in a dress."

"Did they, now?" His voice took on a more menacing tone. "Well, Iverson Hall is private property, and I'm just about fed up with their pathetic complaints. They're nothing but a bunch of bigots and whingers using any excuse to get at me!"

"Mr Iverson, I do have to ask you this, but do you know whether Rupert was bisexual?" Julie asked. "Or if anyone in the village might have thought he was?"

That produced another angry response. "My son made no secret of the fact he loved women," he said. "I've no reason to believe he was gay or bisexual or LGBTQ or whatever you want to call it."

"So have you any thoughts about why these people might want to hurt you by posting this online abuse?"

She heard another lengthy exhale before Dennis responded. "I think I know what this is about, and who's behind it. I want to report this online abuse. It's a hate crime, isn't it?"

"That's what would have to be investigated," said Julie.

The line went silent. Julie imagined Dennis mopping his brow. Then he continued. "As for so-called corruption, this is ancient history. Some years ago, when I was on the planning committee, I was involved in a local building project in Tideburgh with a developer. I obviously declared an interest. Obviously!"

"So what's the problem then?"

"The problem is that rumours have been going on ever since, according to which I leaned on council members to vote in favour of my application. Which is a total and utter lie! I swear that everything was completely above board."

"But why have they cropped up again?" Julie wanted to know.

"It's obvious, isn't it? Tideburgh is under threat from tidal surges and whatnot, and the coast is being eroded in great chunks. You must have seen it — the coastal path has almost disappeared behind Iverson Hall!"

"Yes, I did notice."

"To be honest, I think some of them think that because of my responsibility on the coastal management committee, I've got a conflict of interest, which is completely untrue. All I've done is to tell my officers that I don't want the situation on Blackberry Lane to drag on for years like it did in Happisburgh. I want it expedited!"

"Why? What happened there, then?"

"In Happisburgh, the residents of Beach Road whose property was at immediate risk were offered a plot under a rollback scheme we agreed with the Department of the Environment. They gave us £3 million in funding so that the council could purchase, demolish and replace nine houses. But the whole thing dragged on and at least one of the residents refused to move out."

"Yes, I knew about that. So it's a bit like what's happening here now?"

"Yes, but the fact is that the scheme in Happisburgh was a one-off. Now, the risk in Tideburgh is just as serious, but we don't have the funding to offer the residents an alternative site. So the two occupants at the end of Blackberry Lane are on their own. Their houses are worthless. Of course if residents become homeless, the council has a duty to rehouse them. We've told them to leave on safety grounds and have offered them council housing in another village, but so far they're digging in their heels, God only knows why. If they go on like this for much longer, we'll have to demolish their houses because we're not allowed to let them fall onto the beach. And soon there could be more at risk."

"Oh dear."

"Quite." Julie heard Iverson lighting another cigarette before he continued. "But I'm being blamed for not finding a solution! As if I can persuade the government to cough up, just like that! All this will take time while we work out another financial mechanism. And, believe me, it's complicated." He paused and she heard another long puff.

"Anyway, I've not got time to go into details now, but I can assure you that my mind is focused on the problem because one of these days Iverson Hall itself is going to fall off the cliff. This part of the coast has lost thirty-six houses over two decades, by the way. Not to mention four businesses and the lifeboat station."

"Thanks very much for your time, Mr Iverson," said Julie, jumping in while he drew breath. "We'll be in touch."

She hung up with relief and leaned back in her chair, her face flushed, just at the moment when Clayton arrived with a cup of coffee, which he placed on her desk.

"Great timing," she said.

* * *

Julie spent the rest of the day catching up on the interviews of party guests on the system. A portrait of Rupert Iverson was gradually emerging. She loved how a murder case revealed secrets, sometimes long buried, and sometimes not even known to the victim. It intrigued her that Rupert didn't suspect before his death that Cathy was going to end their relationship, nor had Cathy been aware that he had the same plan.

She read that there was general agreement among the guests that Cathy had rescued him from a downward spiral after the break-up with Bethany. Apart from Terry Monahan, nobody was aware of the reconciliation of Bethany and Rupert, or at least they weren't volunteering the information. Julie wondered how well these friends had actually known Rupert. *Or maybe we're not asking the right questions.*

She thought about how many of her own friends she would invite to a fancy-dress party. She could only muster the number of close friends on one hand, a far cry from twenty-five. She blamed her job for that, as well as her single-mother status, the two conspiring to prevent her having much of a social life, unless she counted the occasional chat about childcare over the fence with her next-door neighbour. But then, if her father was paying for the whole thing like Dennis Iverson had, she'd throw out invitations more widely. Could this be where Rupert had got into trouble? With a relative stranger in their midst who had some sort of hold over him? There had to be somebody at the gathering who could shed light on the murder, surely?

She mentally went through the most common possible motives for murder. So often it came down to jealousy, lust, revenge or robbery. *Maybe Clayton was right about the green-eyed monster?*

She examined the guest list again, particularly Rupert's changes. Bethany's character and that of Cathy had been swapped. Something had obviously happened in their relationships for Bethany to become the secret wife, while Cathy was in the role of the king's earlier favourite. She remembered Cathy describing herself as the 'mistress-in-chief' and therefore being unaware of the switch. What about Bethany? Had Rupert confided in her? And what about the mysterious James Crofton?

She researched the background of the friends on the list. The majority were people the victim had known in his schooldays and were now mostly scattered across Norfolk. Rupert didn't seem to have kept any friends from university in London, apart from Bethany. She wondered whose idea it had been for Rupert to return to Tideburgh, and whether his father had known about his revived relationship with Bethany. Maybe he'd even encouraged it. He'd given them enough signals that he was a big fan. Clearly his parents had been there for Rupert, but maybe too much?

There were no contact details for James Crofton. A search turned up two people by that name living in Norwich. One was a musician and the other an estate agent. Their photos on the internet showed young men in their twenties. She tried to imagine each of them in full make-up and a crinoline dress. Then she remembered what she'd read about Henriette's death: she'd been poisoned. *Could James Crofton's life be in danger?* No, she told herself — Rupert had given James the role of Henriette, and he was dead.

Still, she couldn't help looking online to see who had been accused of administering the fatal dose of poison. It was the Chevalier de Lorraine, the lover of the king's brother. Who had gone to the party in that role? Jonathan Murray, the real-life partner of Brian Mason. Could this be a message from Rupert

Iverson from beyond the grave? This 'court of the Sun King' case was one of the strangest that Julie had ever handled.

She realised with astonishment that it was after six and switched off her computer. Ollie would be on his way home from football. Clayton was still staring at his screen. He must have got the details of Rupert's phone records. Bullard was nowhere to be seen. As usual. He had a knack of disappearing when the jobs he considered drudgery needed to be done.

She noticed Clayton turn round abruptly just as she was getting ready to leave. He came running over to her desk. "We've got the missing cricket bat. A dog walker and his son found it the morning after the party!"

"Wow, where's it been all this time?"

"They found it on the beach beside the sea defences the morning after the party and took it home, of course, but the father brought it in after seeing a story in the *EDP*. The boss doesn't want to make an announcement yet, though, until we get the DNA checked."

That was good news to go home on, she thought, picking up her bag. Perhaps this case was turning in their favour.

* * *

Her upbeat mood didn't last for long. The next morning, Julie's phone rang just as she was about to leave for the nick after Ollie had gone to school. As usual, before she departed, she was double-checking that she'd switched off all the taps, unplugged all the plugs and that all the towels in the bathroom were neatly folded. She traced the ringing to the kitchen counter.

It was Clayton. She could tell from his tone of voice that something had come up.

"Julie, we've got to go back to Tideburgh. I'll see you there."

"Why, what's happened?" she asked.

"A woman's body has been found on the beach. They called it in to us in case there's a connection to the Iverson murder."

CHAPTER TWELVE

The CSI van had somehow managed to manoeuvre onto Tideburgh beach where a small group of rubberneckers had gathered.

The spot where the woman had fallen to her death had been covered with a white forensics tent, while the dog walkers and passers-by were held back by police tape. Julie and Clayton parked in a small car park near the cliffs within moments of each other and took the path down to the beach where their footprints sank into the sand.

A techie emerged from the tent with an evidence bag and Clayton approached.

"DI Clayton and DS Everett," Clayton said. "So lightning can strike twice, then, eh? What do you think happened here?"

"From the state of the body it looks like she fell yesterday evening. It's a thirty-foot drop and she might have had a chance of survival, but her head hit a rock. Her arms were wet from the tide which was up at eight thirty last night. She was found just before high tide this morning. Luckily it didn't come up any higher, otherwise she could have been washed away."

"And what about why she fell?"

"You'd better talk to the CSM about that, guv," the techie said. Clayton looked round and saw the crime scene manager taking notes on a clipboard at the back of the van. Julie followed him over.

"There's some bruising but we'll need to examine the body at the lab to find out what happened exactly," the crime scene manager said. "A dog walker found her."

"Why would anyone go out walking along here after dark?" Julie asked. "I mean, the coastal path is dangerously close to the cliff edge."

"Has she been identified?" Clayton asked.

"Yes." The crime scene manager consulted her notes. "According to the locals she's Iris Haggett. Two Gs, two Ts. Address is Blackberry Lane. Just up there beside the car park," she said. "We're trying to locate the relatives. They're not local, apparently."

Julie recognised the name immediately. "She's one of the residents who's been warned her house is unsafe, guv. Iris Haggett. I'm sure of that."

"Didn't you say there was somebody else as well?"

"Let's see." Julie pulled out her notebook. "Richard Fairbairn."

"Let's take a gander," said Clayton. "And then we'd better get back to the nick."

The two detectives walked past the wooden sea defences on the beach on their way back up to the car park.

"Is this all they've got to protect them from the sea?" Clayton commented.

"Looks like it." Julie pointed towards the cliff. "You see the different colours? Up top where those tufts of grass are, it's a darker brown. That's clay up there. And sand lower down. That's why they're so vulnerable to collapse — the waves cut into the sandy bottom and then the top comes tumbling down. The pub landlord told me that."

They took a footpath up from the beach. Next to the car park, behind thickets of brambles, were two small red-brick bungalows on a pocket of grass. One was only yards from the cliff edge. The other, in the opposite corner, further away from the edge, had a porch constructed from a ramshackle tarpaulin held up by two wooden posts. A rickety shed stood beside it.

"So these are the two residents defying the council?" Clayton asked.

"For now, yes," Julie replied. "But surely it's only a matter of time before the rest of Blackberry Lane falls into the sea. And Iverson Hall with it. Several metres of land are vanishing every year." She turned and saw the manor set back from its paddock and realised that this was the clump of houses on the cliffs that she'd noticed on their first visit.

"But are you suggesting that Dennis Iverson could have something to do with this, because of his role on the council?"

"You mean with Iris Haggett's death? No, not really. Let's face it, he's in mourning for his son. Why on earth would he attack this woman, even if she was making his life difficult? It doesn't make sense. Although he seemed to be blaming the interested parties for posting those horrible things about his house."

"We'd better have another word with him," said Clayton. Julie hoped that it wouldn't be her turn again.

"I wonder which one is Iris Haggett's?" she said. They could hear a dog barking from inside the first house.

Clayton looked at the address the crime scene manager had given him.

"It's the other one." He pointed towards the bungalow by the clifftop.

He knocked on the front door, which faced eastwards. Two large windows were on either side of the door, the painted window frames peeling away in the salt air. Julie peered inside. She could make out a collection of shells on a table piled high with papers. The other room contained a bed and a wardrobe. She went round to the back where potted plants were on the kitchen windowsill, their leaves pressing against the pane. There was no sign of anyone in the house. Driftwood and a pile of tools were scattered untidily on the grass.

Clayton joined her. "Nobody here," he said.

"No. But look at this view. You can see for miles. No wonder they want to stay," she said, stretching out her arms. Looking west, she could see the Happisburgh lighthouse. To the east, the cube of the disused military shelter that she'd visited. In the field beside it, she could make out low brown shapes moving in the stubble.

"Do you see those geese over there?" she said, pointing. "I bet they're the pink-footed ones. Cathy told me they invade the place every winter."

"Remember that for your next pub quiz. Let's see if the neighbour's home — he might know why she was out last night, or when she left." They walked back across the grass, but there was no answer to Julie's knock. The only sound from inside was the dog which was barking itself hoarse.

Their feet crunched on the car park gravel. Clayton slid into his car and wound down the window.

"See you back at the nick. We could grab a butty in the canteen if you fancy."

Julie was looking in the direction of the beach, a frown on her face. "That cricket bat . . . I wonder how it ended up by the sea defences. Do you think it was high tide and the killer chucked it off the cliffs thinking it would wash out to sea?"

"Could be," said Clayton. "And then, luckily for us, it got stuck on the defences when the tide went down. Fifi's got it now, anyway. If you get back before I do, mine's a bacon butty!"

* * *

Julie pushed through the swing doors into the cafeteria and saw Clayton at their usual corner table ensconced with a cup of coffee and crispy bacon peeking out of his white bread sandwich.

She ordered a cappuccino and joined him. She'd wait until lunchtime for a snack.

"So what else is new then, Julie?" he asked.

"Not much. But do you think there might be a possible gay aspect to the murder, after all? I mean the hidden code for the party guests, James Crofton as Henriette, and those comments online — about Rupert being killed after an orgy . . . Or if the place is a regular feature of a hard party scene, well, was chemsex involved? Could Rupert have somehow been—? What if it was a lovers' tiff that turned violent?"

Clayton wiped his lips with a paper napkin and put down his half-eaten sandwich. "This is good, by the way," he murmured. "I think it probably started with a rumour in the village which is being fuelled by social media," he went on. "People think they can get away with anything online these days in the name of free speech, don't they? And does anyone say Rupert was gay, or bi? Or into drugs?"

"So far, neither his girlfriend nor his dad," said Julie. She took a long sip of her coffee. "But I suppose it's even possible that his killer might have wanted to out Rupert against his will . . ."

"Well, the tox results showed he was clean, don't forget." He pushed his plate away. "Reet. Anyway, what are we doing about this other guy in a frock? He's the one who holds the key to this. It's only when we get to him that we'll find out whether the hypothesis about a gay guest murdering Rupert is bollocks."

Julie observed Clayton from over her coffee cup. If she'd been asked, she'd have had to admit that he was probably homophobic. And racist, too, like a lot of policemen. She'd picked up on his awkward body language in their contacts with a gay music conductor in an earlier case, and wished she'd spoken out when he'd mocked the musician's slightly camp demeanour. Maybe as a straight guy from a socially conservative background he felt uncomfortable around gay men. But he also had a problem with women, particularly those in positions of power. She gathered he'd been bullied by the women in his family, which might partly explain his attitude, but still that added up to quite a package of prejudice. Like most people, Clayton was a child of his era. But he didn't seem interested in changing with the times. She suspected that Bullard, being younger, would be more broad-minded, but she knew that discrimination was still a live issue in the police force.

Mentally ticking off her police colleagues, she realised that even now, none of them was openly gay and that she only knew one officer who wasn't white. That was Lucy Jayewardene, whose parents were from Sri Lanka. Everyone called her Lucy Jay, because they said they couldn't pronounce her name.

She put down her cup. "I've found out there are two James Croftons in Norwich, a musician and an estate agent."

Clayton reacted strangely when she mentioned the estate agent.

"Do you know which estate agency?" he asked.

"Fawcett's."

"Not on Unthank Road?" he asked. Julie knew that road ran through the 'Golden Triangle' where Clayton lived.

"No. It's one near the castle, I think. Why, do you know it?"

He shrugged. She waited. He cleared his throat.

"It's just that, you know, my girlfriend, well she's at the branch on Unthank Road. They've got this big sign up, *Fawcett's The One to Trust*. It could have been a bit awkward, that's all . . ."

"Really, why?"

He was fiddling with something in his jacket pocket and seemed ill at ease. He eventually said, "Nothing special, I probably shouldn't have mentioned it but she's not really my girlfriend anymore. Or at least not at the moment, anyway."

"Oh. I'm sorry." Julie had often wondered whether Clayton would get back together with his ex-wife, who worked in neurology at Norwich Hospital. That much she knew. It had taken him a long time to get over their divorce, apparently, but he'd seemed to settle down with this girlfriend over the past year or so. She thought better of asking whether he wanted to talk about it. She didn't even know the woman's name.

But she pressed on regardless.

"Didn't you say she was in the choir at the Norwich Festival Orchestra?" she asked. "The other James Crofton is a violinist."

"Really?" said Clayton. "I don't suppose that would matter so much, even if it turned out he was in the orchestra — the musicians tend to stick to themselves, socially. Anyway, let's see which Crofton was at the party. Shall I ask Bullard to check when we get back?"

"No, that's fine, I can go," she said. After all, she'd done all the legwork. Why hand over to Bullard now?

CHAPTER THIRTEEN

Julie felt a prickle of excitement when Clayton passed by her desk to let her know that Bethany Price was waiting downstairs. It was their chance to weigh up this beauty that everyone found so alluring.

"Kev's come through with the goods," Clayton told her on the way down. "The interesting thing, too, is that on the night of the party, Rupert didn't get any calls or messages apart from one. It was from Bethany at seven o'clock."

"So you mean . . . ?"

"I mean that the killer didn't get in touch with him by phone to get him to go downstairs. So either it was a prearranged meeting by the pool or the attacker got in touch with him another way, or it was chance," said Clayton. "Anyway, let's see what she's got to say for herself."

Bethany had the confident look of a young professional and was soberly dressed in a trouser suit that flattered her trim figure. Her red hair was loosely tied back, revealing her alabaster complexion. She was flicking through a file on a chair in reception and looked up when the two detectives approached. Clayton did the introductions and led her into an interview room.

"Let's just run through your particulars, Ms Price," he said, switching on the tape. "Thank you for attending voluntarily. You've come straight from work, have you?"

"Yes. I'm in the Norwich town planning department. We've got quite a bit of work on at the moment." Her voice was rich and warm. It was immediately obvious what Rupert would have seen in her.

They didn't interrupt until she gave her address in Norwich. Julie asked, "And we understand that you live at that address with Mr Jacob Morrison, is that correct?"

"Yes." She didn't elaborate further.

Clayton let Julie take the lead. She started by asking about Bethany's relationship with Rupert Iverson at university.

"Could you tell us why the two of you split up?" Julie asked. "It seems to have had quite an effect on him."

"Well, that's rather personal," she said.

She doesn't know what's coming, Julie thought.

Clayton said, "Ms Price, we're investigating the suspected murder of your former boyfriend. Of course it's personal."

"Well, I just felt that we were too young to settle down, which is what Rupert wanted. He told me that I was 'the one'."

"And what about you?" asked Julie.

"I don't know. Well, I thought he could be, yes, but we had our whole lives in front of us and I didn't want to be pinned down at the age of twenty-one."

Clayton followed up. "But we understand that you got back together recently. Does that mean that you'd decided that he was your soulmate after all?"

Bethany's eyes widened in surprise. "How do you know that, Inspector?"

"The two of you were exchanging lots of text messages." Before she could react further, he added, "In fact, on the night he died, there was a message from you just before you went to the party. Could you tell us what that was about?"

Bethany began to tug a strand of her lustrous hair from behind an ear, glancing from side to side. Julie remembered the ginger hair found by Cathy in their bed.

"Oh, I think I just said I was looking forward to seeing him."

"Is that all?" Bethany stared at Julie as though weighing up whether the questions about the messages might be a trap.

"Yes. I might have said I was *excited* about seeing him. It was his birthday, after all. But I don't remember exactly."

Her eyes moistened, but she blinked back tears.

Clayton picked up the questioning. "Do you want to take a moment, Ms Price?"

"No, that's fine."

"We also understand that you planned to end your relationship with Jacob Morrison."

Her slim figure tautened on the chair. She kept holding onto the strand of hair like a talisman.

"Is that correct?" Clayton persisted.

"Yes," she said in a low voice. "I told Jacob that night."

"On the night of the party? While you were there?"

"No, before we set off."

"And did you inform him about your relationship with Rupert Iverson?"

"Yes, I did."

"How did he react? Why did he decide to go to the party?" Julie asked.

"He was pretty angry. About the deception, I suppose. I wouldn't say he was distraught, more angry. But some of his friends would be there too, and he wanted to see them."

"Is it likely that people at the party were aware of what had been going on with Rupert?"

"I don't think so, no. I certainly didn't tell anyone. I didn't want Cathy to be hurt."

"But it's possible that Jacob confided in these friends while he was there."

"Yes. I suppose so. But you'd better ask him."

Julie leaned forward. "How did Rupert strike you at the party? Did he seem OK? Preoccupied or worried?"

Bethany paused to think. "No. Quite the opposite. He was in high spirits. He seemed fine, actually . . . in fact, he told me at one point that he had a surprise for me."

"A surprise? What kind of surprise?" asked Julie.

"I don't know. He said it was a 'nice' surprise and that he'd tell me after the party."

What new secret was this?

Clayton leaned forward. "Ms Price, did you mention this surprise to anyone at the party?"

"No, of course not. It was between Rupert and me. Why?"

"Because we believe that Rupert's killer, or killers, were trying to obtain information from him. So it's possible that they were aware of his secret," Clayton went on.

Bethany's hazel eyes stared straight at Clayton. But she simply repeated that she'd told nobody. "And I didn't try to guess what the surprise would be, as he was going to tell me afterwards," she said.

"Did you and Jacob leave together, or separately?" Julie asked.

"We left together at about one in the morning. One of Jacob's friends had taken us there, and he brought us back to Norwich."

Clayton cleared his throat before asking, "Once you were back home, did you share a bed?"

"Well, no. Like I said, I'd ended things with Jacob earlier that night."

"I see. And could you describe the sleeping arrangements?"

"It's a town house. The master bedroom is on the top floor. That's where I slept. Jacob was in the spare room on the first floor."

"And would it be possible for the person on the first floor to leave the house without the person on the top floor hearing?"

Bethany clearly realised what Clayton was driving at. She paused before replying and stopped playing with her hair.

"In theory, yes. But if you're suggesting that Jacob went back to Tideburgh to kill Rupert, in the middle of the night, you're barking up the wrong tree. Are we finished here?" She reached for her bag.

Julie cut in. "Just one more thing, please. Who did you dress as for the party?"

"I went as Madame de Maintenon," she said breezily.

"The king's secret wife, correct?"

The question punctured Bethany's poise. "Oh. Yes, I believe she was."

"Were you aware that Rupert had originally picked another role for you?" Julie asked. Bethany frowned. She clearly hadn't had an inkling that she'd been raised in Rupert's Louis XIV pantheon.

"No I didn't, actually," she said. "Who was it?"

Julie hesitated before looking at Clayton, who closed his file.

"I don't think it's relevant to the investigation to disclose that," he said. They got up to escort Bethany out.

"I can see who was wearing the trousers in that relationship," Julie commented, once she was gone.

"You mean her and Jacob Morrison?" Clayton asked.

"No. Her and Rupert."

Clayton grinned. "It's clear, though, that Jacob Morrison had every reason to be angry with Rupert Iverson on the night of the murder."

"Yes, but what about the surprise she mentioned?" said Julie. "Rupert was waterboarded for a reason. It wasn't a spur-of-the-moment thing. What was his secret that they wanted him to reveal?"

CHAPTER FOURTEEN

Julie peered past the housing ads through the window of Fawcett's estate agency on Castle Meadow to see who was inside.

There didn't seem to be any clients, but there were three agents at their desks, one on the phone and the other two consulting their computers. Only one was a man, of slim build and in his twenties. He must be the man she was here to speak to — a couple of phone calls had established that this was the James Crofton who had attended the party.

Julie went in and approached him.

"Are you looking for a rental?" he asked.

In a quiet voice she asked if he was James Crofton and took out her warrant card. "It's about Rupert Iverson," she said. "Is there somewhere we can talk?"

He glanced at the others to see whether either of his colleagues were watching, then got up and said loudly, "Anyone want anything?" The others barely looked up from what they were doing, and he led her into a small room at the back, where a Nespresso machine and a kettle stood on a counter.

"Can I get you a tea or coffee?" he asked. He was the same height as Julie and dressed in a suit jacket and jeans.

His tie was loose around his neck. Julie couldn't help trying to imagine him in a wig, make-up and a frock.

"Er, no thanks, I'm fine," she said, taking out her notebook. "I wanted to ask you why you went as a woman to Rupert's party. It might be important for the murder investigation."

"Did I do something wrong?" he asked. He seemed nervous, and his voice began to shake. "We're all very upset about what happened. He was too young to die."

"No, no, it's just that we're trying to piece together Rupert's relationships. Was he gay?"

"Rups? Gay? God, no," he blurted out.

"So why . . . ?"

"Why did I go as Henrietta? Basically, it was to humour Rupert, who gave me the role. He knew that Brian and I were having a fling, and I guess he wanted to play a prank on Brian."

"OK. Understood. But Brian is with Jonathan Murray, isn't he?"

"Yes, that's the point!" he exclaimed. "But obviously neither Brian nor I want Jonathan to know. So I steered clear of Jonathan during the party, and I made myself scarce apart from the odd nod and wink with Rups and Brian. Rupert admired my eyelashes."

"Eyelashes?"

"Falsies, darling," he said. He took a phone from his jacket pocket and swiped through photos before holding it out to Julie.

"Stunning." She smiled. The young man standing beside her was unrecognisable in the photo.

"So he was a bit of a prankster, was he, Rupert?" she asked, handing back the phone. "That seems rather cruel. What if Jonathan had figured out what was going on between you and Brian?"

"Well, that would have been a disaster, of course. They've been together for ages. Luckily, everyone said that my disguise was totally convincing. I was told that I danced a mean minuet. A couple of male courtiers even tried chatting me up. I told them that I was a married lady, but I didn't tell anyone I was Henriette in case someone knew about her being married to the king's brother. It was a fun night."

"Henriette also became the king's mistress, didn't she? So what about you and Rupert?"

"Someone's been doing her homework!" he exclaimed. "Nothing going on there, no. Definitely not."

Julie found herself warming to James. She wondered whether to mention Henriette's unfortunate demise, but asked instead, "How many of the guests did you know?"

"A few of them from school days. Terry took that photo."

"And was Brian also a friend from school days?"

"Not really. We both went to Wymondham but he's a bit older than I am. I recognised him when we met on Grindr a few months ago. But we bumped into Rups in Norwich one night when we were walking Brian's dog. After that, Brian asked him to invite me to the party. Bit of a risk-taker, is Brian." He grinned.

"Did you see much of Rupert in the run-up to the big day?"

"Not much. But we did catch up with him a few days before. He wanted to discuss the costume list with Brian, and I trotted along too."

"Did he mention Bethany's role?"

"You mean her promotion? From royal mistress to secret wife? Brilliant!"

"And if you were aware of this identity change, would you presume that others were as well?"

"Probably everyone was, apart from poor Cathy, I suspect," said James, shaking his head. "Secrets and lies, eh? In a way it was a clever kind of coming-out party for the two of them, Bethany and Rups. Hiding in plain sight, you know?"

"And Jacob Morrison?"

"I don't suppose Jacob was all that happy about it, you're right. The poor boy was sulking at the party. But I must say that the rest of us were pleased about Rups and Bethany being back together again. He was destroyed after they split up. He'd have been a brilliant architect if he'd qualified." He waved a hand in the air. "Anyway, he seems to have made a go of it at the market gardening. I've seen their stuff in my local supermarket here in Norwich."

"Apart from Jacob, can you think of anyone else at the party who might have an axe to grind against Rupert?" Julie persisted.

"Honestly, if you ask me straight out like that, there's nobody that comes to mind. I've been thinking about that since he was killed. And I can't imagine that Jacob would do a thing like that. I mean, hitting someone over the head with a cricket bat before leaving them to die in the pool?"

"We're still hoping forensics will come through," said Julie.

James nodded, and looked at his watch. "Are you sure you don't want anything to drink?"

Julie declined for a second time and put her notebook away. She gave him her card, saying, "If you think of anything else that could help us find who murdered your friend, please get in touch."

* * *

The upstairs bedroom light was on when Julie turned into her drive.

She remained in the car for a moment while she called Paul, her former partner, to arrange for him to pick up Ollie at the weekend. Both of them were police officers and, with Paul based in Ipswich, their plans had frequently fallen through of late. Ollie would be disappointed if Paul didn't make it this time, she thought. He'd promised to take his son to see the Canaries who were playing at home on Saturday.

Her own relationship with Paul remained tense. She hated herself for picking up on perceived slurs but couldn't help it. He was simply exploiting her own guilt about her feelings of being a bad mother. And his studied calm did nothing but annoy her. Sometimes she felt like shaking him to obtain some kind of reaction. She wondered how his girlfriend, Meredith, who was also in the force and the reason for their separation, dealt with him. But he was a good dad, she had to admit.

He picked up straight away. "Hi, Julie. You OK?" he asked.

"Just got home. What about you? Are you still on for this weekend?" She was aware that the last question might be betraying some nervousness.

"Yeah. Still on," he said. "But can I confirm the details later?"

He was always doing this. It was irritating. She sighed. Once again, she wouldn't be able to make plans for herself until the last minute.

"OK. But when will you know?"

"Say, Friday? I've got a fair bit on at the moment."

You and me both.

"Well, Ollie's really looking forward to Saturday," she said. "He talks about nothing else at the moment, apart from tokens and badges for his damned video games."

"Oh yes, I've got the tickets."

She rang off and went inside with the shopping. She took off her jacket, left the bags on the kitchen counter and went up the first few stairs. Ollie's door was closed and she could hear the tick-tock rhythm of his video game.

She hesitated for a second then went up and knocked on the door, poking her head round. Two heads turned round from the computer. Ollie waved, in a way that she took as a dismissal.

"Downstairs in ten minutes, OK?" she said.

He muttered something to his pal and they turned their backs on her. She resisted a strong temptation to shout.

"Are you staying for dinner, Jack?" she asked.

"No thanks, Mrs Everett, I'm going in a minute," Jack replied, with a sideways smirk at Ollie.

She went back outside to double-check that she'd locked the car door, then, having reassured herself that all was well, she checked the front door lock and returned to the kitchen to prepare their macaroni cheese. It was one of Ollie's favourite meals. She took out a bottle of Chardonnay from the fridge and poured herself a glass. *Here goes another evening in front of the TV.*

She switched on Netflix and found *Versailles*. The series had three seasons. That felt like too much of a commitment, and in any case she couldn't watch it with Ollie. She took out her phone and googled the show. She read that it was known for its 'raunchy sex scenes'. It was supposed to run to four seasons but was cancelled after three because of declining ratings. Maybe people could have too much of a good thing.

It was at times like this she missed companionship. Not just anybody, but a partner who could stimulate, support and comfort her with balm for the soul. When Ollie was at primary school she'd briefly got together with one of his teachers, who'd been intimidated by her being a detective. His "are you going to arrest me?" jokes soon wore thin. Although she had much more in common with her colleagues, most of them were married, including the office flirt, whose advances she'd ignored. Those who weren't — including Clayton, whose physique reminded her of a teddy bear — she didn't find attractive.

Anyway, it would be quite a challenge these days to be in a relationship while an eleven-year-old was in the next-door bedroom, she thought. No wonder all her attention was focused on her job. Yet she never seemed to get the praise and attention that someone like Bullard did, despite his laziness. Could it be because she wasn't dashing and male?

Her thoughts turned to Bethany Price. Had she told Rupert during the birthday party that she'd finished with Jacob? The two of them were obviously planning a new life together. How many of the guests had behaved like hypocrites, while keeping up appearances in Cathy's presence?

She took another sip of her wine, leaning on the kitchen counter lost in her thoughts. It was only the smell of cheese burning under the grill that brought her back to reality.

CHAPTER FIFTEEN

The next morning, Clayton came over to Julie's workstation wearing a look of thunder.

"Jacob Morrison can't come in till tonight," he said. "And he's bringing a solicitor. Bethany must have warned him."

"Well, he does work in the City, doesn't he?" she said. "We'll have to interview him under caution, guv."

"You know what that means, though, don't you? No comment, no comment, no sodding comment."

Julie sensed that he was casting round for a wastepaper basket to kick. But they were saved by the sight of Bligh walking through the detective suite in their direction.

They both looked at her expectantly.

"Morning, boss," said Clayton.

"I've just had a conversation with Dr Blackhurst. About Iris Haggett. We can't record accidental death until we've cleared up what happened. And we're still trying to trace her relatives. Her head injuries suggest that she crashed onto the beach at speed. Her neck was broken in the fall."

"You mean she might have been pushed?" Clayton asked.

"We can't rule it out," said Bligh. "That's what we have to find out. Strikes me she was running when she fell off the cliff. And she was lying there all night before she was found the next morning. So what was that woman doing out in the dark? And who, or what, was she running from?"

"The thing is, could it be linked to the Rupert Iverson case?" said Clayton. The three of them looked at each other in silence.

"Iris Haggett was a middle-aged woman, living alone, with no apparent connection to the Iversons," said Bligh.

"Yes, ma'am, but there's a connection to Dennis Iverson because of a dispute over her home, which is in danger of falling into the sea. He's the chair of the coastal management committee on the district council, you see," Julie explained.

Clayton asked Bligh whether forensics had any positive ID yet from the cricket bat recovered from the sea.

"They have some touch DNA that they're working on. Of course the seawater has eroded some of the evidence, just like the chemicals in the pool will have affected the analysis to some extent. But luckily, because of the limited time that the bat was submerged, they should be able to recover something useable."

"That's good," said Clayton.

"I'll let you crack on, then." She turned on her heel.

"Are you going to speak to Dennis Iverson?" Julie asked Clayton.

"I'll give him a ring. Can you go back to Tideburgh to talk to Haggett's neighbour, Richard Fairbairn?"

"Sure."

"Do you want to take Bullard?" Clayton asked.

"That's OK, guv, I'll be fine. He's probably had enough of dogs after being nipped by that pug."

* * *

By the time Julie reached the coast, the wind was gathering and clouds raced across the big sky. Only a couple of cars were in the car park.

She approached Fairbairn's bungalow, next door to Iris Haggett's. Gnarled driftwood stood by the entrance, where the makeshift canopy had been erected over plastic matting. The tarpaulin was flapping in the breeze. A garden broom stood in the corner next to a folding plastic chair. A couple of painting canvases were propped up outside the door beside an easel, their backs towards her.

If Fairbairn cleared away the brambles, he'd have a clear view along the coast for his painting, she thought. As it was, she had the impression of a man who'd barricaded himself in.

Loud barking made her jump just as she was about to knock on the door. She heard a man's voice telling the dog to shut up, before a big man in his fifties pulled open the door, holding a wiry mongrel by its collar. The man's paunch was covered by a heavy sweater. He had a ruddy complexion and an unkempt beard. Julie caught a glimpse of a pile of beer cans on the floor behind him. He'd be attractive if he hadn't let himself go to seed, she thought.

"Mr Fairbairn?" Julie held up her warrant card. "Detective Sergeant Julie Everett, Anglian Constabulary."

"Just a minute." He pushed the dog inside and stepped onto the grass, closing the door behind him. His hands were smudged with traces of paint. "What do you want?"

"We're investigating the death of Iris Haggett, who fell from the cliffs two nights ago."

"What do you want to know?" His voice was gruff.

Julie took out her notebook. "We understand that she lived alone, is that correct?"

"Oh. Yes. She has a daughter, who visits from time to time. But she's not local."

"I see. Actually, I'm wondering why she would have been out alone at night," said Julie.

"Why, do you think she'd ask me for permission? She's a grown woman and frankly I don't know what she got up to at night." That appeared to be the end of that particular line of questioning.

"Can you think of any reason why someone would want her dead?" That question seemed to strike a chord.

"I can, but I don't think that even he would go that far," he said.

"Who's 'he'?" Julie asked. In the face of his silence, she pressed on, saying, "I understand you're in negotiations with the district council about moving away from the cliff edge."

Richard Fairbairn frowned. "Negotiations? What negotiations? Iverson sent his officers over here and basically told Iris and me to our faces at a public meeting that we're being evicted because our houses are unsafe. Do you know what he said in front of everybody else? 'It's only like grief . . . you'll get over it.' This is how we're treated! I could have punched him. As far as I'm concerned, my family has lived here on this lane for generations, so I'm not budging, and I told Iverson that."

"You mean Dennis Iverson? But he's local himself."

"He's not local. He might have a house here but he's not *from* here. I think he's from Essex or somewhere like that." And then, just in case Julie hadn't completely understood his point, Richard concluded, "We don't like outsiders round here."

It wasn't the first time she'd heard this in the Norfolk villages on her patch. Sometimes obtaining information was like prising open an oyster.

"Were you referring to Dennis Iverson just now, when I asked you who would kill Iris Haggett?"

Richard Fairbairn shrugged his shoulders. "Maybe I was, maybe I wasn't. I don't know who killed her." He ruminated for a moment longer before exclaiming, "And he's such a flashy bastard! Have you seen his car?"

"The Rolls?"

He nodded. "And those parties. They put up tents in the field, they have weddings and parties, you can imagine the noise and the mess they make in the summer. The car park is overflowing so they park along the lane here, ruining flower-beds and the like. I reckon they shouldn't be allowed to disturb the peace in a village like ours. I mean, it's not Glastonbury."

"Are you aware that some villagers have been posting complaints about the parties on the Iverson Hall website?" Julie asked.

"I wouldn't be surprised. A few of us got up a petition to try to get a midnight curfew imposed, but Iverson ignored us. I don't know about complaints online though. I don't have a computer here. Never needed one. Now, if there's nothing else, I need to get on with my work."

Julie tried one last question. "But, just to come back to Iris Haggett. I suppose that she was upset about Mr Iverson too, if she'd been told to leave her property."

"Oh, yes, of course she was upset. Ask anyone round here!"

He heaved his shoulders before adding: "The point is that Iverson knows we're screwed. Everybody on Blackberry Lane is screwed, in fact. He told us that there's no deal to be had with the government like they did in Happisburgh a few years ago. Our houses are worthless. So here, either you wait until your house falls off the cliff, like I am, or you bugger off somewhere else at your own expense. So either way, we're screwed."

That's very sad. But it's not Dennis Iverson's fault.

"Didn't I see that there's a house that had a 'Sold' sign in the garden, though? What do you mean about their houses being worthless?"

"Ha!" he said. "You're right. Some people are able to sell because the buyers have made the calculation that with monthly rents here of about £800 to £1,000, if they can pay less than £360,000 to buy a house that will be destroyed in thirty years' time it's worth their while. So, yes, one or two people on Blackberry Lane can sell up. But it's too late for me to do that here. And like I said, I don't want to move, anyway."

Julie put away her notebook. "And what's your line of work? Do you paint, then?"

He glanced at the easel propped against the wall under the porch. "How did you guess?" He clearly didn't want to engage in small talk. "I'm a carpenter by trade."

Julie thanked him for his time and asked for his phone number. He told her he didn't have a phone. It wasn't the first time she'd heard that, either, in this neck of the woods.

CHAPTER SIXTEEN

Jacob Morrison didn't blink when Clayton warned him that the interview was taking place under caution.

"Do you understand, Mr Morrison?"

He nodded.

"For the tape, please?" Clayton glanced up at the corner of the interview room, where the camera was blinking. Bligh would be watching in her office.

"Yes, understood," Jacob replied. He was quite the City gent, in a sharp suit and pink shirt, and his voice was clipped. His solicitor, old enough to be his mother, had taken her place opposite Julie at the table. Her name was Catherine McKinsey and she was a familiar face on the Norwich legal circuit.

"Could you give us your exact movements on the night of Rupert Iverson's party, Mr Morrison?" said Clayton.

"Starting from when?"

"From the moment you arrived at Iverson Hall."

"Right. Well, Bethany and I were among the last to arrive, I think. A friend of ours drove us there, Toby Mallett. That's double T. We got there a bit after nine, I recall. Then Bethany and I stayed until around midnight and went home."

"Was there any particular reason why you were late arriving?" Clayton asked.

Jacob sighed. "You'll have heard that Bethany ended our relationship that evening. We had a bit of a row, which meant we were late leaving the house."

"What was the row about?" Julie asked.

"Well, obviously about the fact that she was leaving me for her ex-boyfriend."

"Rupert Iverson."

"Yes."

"And how did you feel about that?"

"How do you think I felt?" Jacob was beginning to lose his studied cool. "I was angry, of course, because she'd been cheating on me and this was the first I'd heard about it. She admitted the relationship with Rupert Iverson —" he practically spat out the name — "had been going on for weeks."

"So why did you go to the party?" Julie asked. "Bethany could have gone on her own, couldn't she?"

"We both decided that it would attract more attention if she was on her own than not. To be honest, as I had my costume, I was pretty keen on going. Probably not the best decision I ever took, but there you are," he said, with a sideways glance at the solicitor.

"OK. Did you confide in anyone about the situation with Bethany when you got there?" asked Clayton.

"I told Toby, obviously, but only when we got to the party. He was pretty fed up because we kept him waiting outside for us in his Jag dressed up as Fabien Marchal. He said he felt ridiculous sitting there in his costume — not that his was particularly ostentatious, compared to the rest of us."

"Thanks for that information." Clayton's voice was heavy with sarcasm.

"Who did you go as?" Julie asked, risking Clayton's annoyance.

"Louvois," Jacob replied.

"Who was he?"

"Well, ironically, he was Louis XIV's right-hand man."

"Why ironically? Because you weren't very friendly with Rupert Iverson?"

Jacob seemed to realise he may have said too much. His eyes slid across to the solicitor again, but she was silent.

"I didn't know him very well. I'd only met him through Bethany," he replied. "So no, I wouldn't say I was ever particularly friendly with Rupert."

"And during the party, did you say anything to Rupert about him and Bethany?"

"No, I didn't. In fact I didn't speak to him for the whole evening. As you can imagine, I didn't have particularly warm feelings for him that night."

"Did you tell anyone else about Bethany and Rupert, apart from Toby?" Clayton asked.

"I mentioned it to a couple of friends, David Jolly and Steve Palmer."

"Did you discuss taking revenge on either Bethany or Rupert?" Clayton asked.

"Of course not! What do you take me for?" The solicitor leaned across to Jacob and whispered something to him. He took a moment to compose himself.

"But you did tell them how upset you were?" said Julie.

"Yes."

Clayton looked at his file and continued, "Let's return to when you got home. Toby dropped you and Bethany off together, correct?"

"Yes," came the reply.

"At what time would that be?"

"It must have been about one thirty, I suppose."

"Where did you sleep that night?"

There was a pause. "In the spare room."

"That's on the first floor, beneath the main bedroom where Bethany slept?"

"Yes."

"And did you leave that room for any reason during the night?" Clayton asked.

"I might have got up to go to the loo. In fact I think I did. But that was it." Jacob was staring at Clayton. He knew exactly what he was driving at.

"OK. So you remained at the house until the next morning?"

"Yes," said Jacob.

"Thank you, Mr Morrison. That will be all for now." Clayton shut his file.

They watched him leave with McKinsey.

"Bloody posho," said Clayton as soon as they were out of earshot. Julie smiled.

"We've got contact details for Jacob Morrison's friends, have we?" he asked.

"I'm sure our people have interviewed them already, yes. But we'll need to go back to them in the light of what he just said to see if they confirm his version," said Julie. "Do you think he's telling the truth?"

"Unfortunately, yes. If he'd gone back to the house to attack Rupert, he'd have had to leave not long after returning to Norwich. Doesn't stack up, does it? And how would he have got there? In a cab?" Clayton stood up. "Let's grab a decent cup of coffee."

CHAPTER SEVENTEEN

The whiff of Clayton's favourite morning snack drifted through the swing doors as they entered the cafeteria.

Julie watched him wander over to the food counter to fetch a bacon sandwich while she helped herself to a teabag and a cup full of hot water. They found their table beside a wilting ficus plant which had seen better days and nodded to colleagues as they pulled up their chairs.

"Did you get anything out of Dennis Iverson?" Julie asked, slinging her handbag onto the back of her seat.

"He's all fired up about those postings on Facebook. He says they're dragging their feet about deleting them. He couldn't stand Iris Haggett, that much is clear. He blamed her and Richard Fairbairn for stirring up the whole of Blackberry Lane against him."

"And Fairbairn is stirring up the locals about the parties at Iverson Hall, too. There's obviously bad blood between them. But you don't think Iverson might have . . ."

"Murdered her? I still can't see it, can you?" said Clayton.

"No. But what about the online abuse? Do you think those messages constitute a hate crime?"

"Not hate crime because where's the crime? Based on what we saw I'd record it as a hate incident — or as you say, common or garden online abuse. But unless we find out who wrote the comments, we won't know if they're relevant to the murder."

"Fair enough. But when people get worked up online, it can lead to really bad things happening. It's pernicious. And what's more, it could complicate our investigation."

"True enough."

Clayton finished wolfing down his sandwich and licked his fingers. Julie reached into her bag to make sure she hadn't missed a message from Ollie.

"How's your lad enjoying school?" Clayton enquired as though reading her thoughts. He scrunched up his paper napkin and dropped it onto his plate.

"So far, so good," she said. "But he's reached the age where he answers back and treats me like a maid. I only see him at mealtimes. The rest of the time he's up in his room on his computer with his mates."

"What, video games?" Clayton wouldn't know what she was talking about if she mentioned *Fortnite*. "Sure they're not up to no good?"

"I hope not. I've got the parental controls on," she replied, sipping her tea. "But I feel like I'm on his case all the time. Of course he ignores me. I supposed he's reached that age and I'll have to get used to it. He's not even a teenager yet."

"Good luck with that." Clayton grinned.

"What about you? Everything OK?" Julie asked.

Clayton didn't reply straight away. Maybe there was still *trouble at t'mill*, as he would say, with the girlfriend.

"It's my dad," he said eventually. "I might have to go up. I don't know if I told you he's in a care home —" she shook her head — "but he's in hospital after a stroke and they don't know how long he'll last. It sounds serious, anyway. I always thought it would be lung cancer that would get him."

"Oh dear, I'm so sorry to hear that," she said. "Does he smoke?"

Clayton smiled grimly. "Of course."

"Are you going to rush up?"

"It's just a question of when."

"Have you got brothers and sisters?" As soon as she asked the question she remembered his hated sister who had died. "Sorry," she said, quickly.

"That's OK. No, it's just me now. But I can't take time off work unless, or until, he takes a turn for the worse. Not with these two cases on." He shrugged his shoulders and picked up his coffee.

"Are you sure? You could take a few days off or even compassionate leave. I think we need more than a few days to crack the Rupert Iverson case. There's all this painstaking stuff to work through."

He shook his head, signalling that there was no question of him taking any time off. The moment had passed for any more personal confessions. Julie noticed that his sandy hair was receding steadily and that soon he'd be completely bald. *A balding teddy bear.*

His forehead creased into a frown. "You know what, Julie? Either someone's covering something up or we're just not asking the right questions."

"You could say that about a lot of murder cases, guv," she said with a smile.

He nodded slowly. "But there's another thing. I've been thinking about what you said."

What pearl of wisdom might he be referring to, she wondered.

"I'm talking about what happened to Iris Haggett. You said that it wouldn't make any sense for Dennis Iverson to physically attack her. That's right. But if Richard Fairbairn is so wound up about losing his house, and has a personal grudge against Dennis Iverson, it might be the other way round."

"What do you mean?" she asked, frowning.

"What I mean is those people might want to hurt Dennis Iverson. And how might they be able to do that? By harming the person who means the most to him, namely his son, Rupert."

Julie's eyes opened wide. "Richard Fairbairn might have killed Rupert?"

"Why not? That would be a motive, wouldn't it, to get at the father?" His phone on the table buzzed and he picked it up. "It's Bligh. She wants us in the incident room. We can discuss this upstairs."

* * *

Bligh had her back to them and was writing something on the board where photos, maps and names had been pinned. She turned to face the team as the room began to fill.

"I want to make sure that we're not missing something here," she said. "I've heard that the *Eastern Daily Press* is making a connection between the deaths of Rupert Iverson and Iris Haggett. They could be jumping to conclusions, of course, but it's true that two deaths in a small village where nothing ever happens might be too much of a coincidence."

Julie looked across at Clayton, who had an air of studied surprise. Had he slipped any information to the crime correspondent on the *EDP*? He returned her gaze unblinkingly before responding to Bligh.

"DS Everett and I were just discussing this, ma'am," he said. "We think there's a possibility that Rupert's attacker might have been targeting Dennis Iverson by hurting his son. And there are at least two villagers with a big grudge against Iverson senior: Iris Haggett, the deceased woman, and her neighbour Richard Fairbairn. You'll be aware that they've both been warned by the district council's coastal management committee, which Dennis Iverson chairs, that they must leave their homes which are at risk of falling into the sea. And Iverson doesn't seem to be handling it in a very tactful way, to say the least. There's a grudge match between them."

"I see," said Bligh. "So that would be a possible motive. And these are the people living right here, by the cliffs, correct?" She turned back to the board where a detailed map of Tideburgh had been fixed next to a satellite picture.

"That's right, ma'am. So they're only a few hundred yards from Iverson Hall, at the end of Blackberry Lane," said Julie. "Richard Fairbairn says that Iris Haggett was very upset. Her house is now worthless, after all. I suppose it's possible that she might have committed suicide by throwing herself off the cliff. Although I don't know if a fall would be fatal from that height if you just dropped onto the beach."

"Right," said Bligh. "Iris Haggett is dead and Richard Fairbairn sounds like the ringleader in the campaign against Dennis Iverson. I'll get a search warrant for Fairbairn's place and let's bring him in for questioning. But we're still no closer to finding out what happened to the woman."

CHAPTER EIGHTEEN

Two days later, Julie parked outside a secondary school near Tideburgh. Over the weekend, the investigation into Iris Haggett's death had taken a new direction.

Richard Fairbairn had been interviewed under caution at a local police station. During the session, he had volunteered that Iris Haggett had "got in a lather" about teenagers playing in the disused gun battery in the field not far from Blackberry Lane. She'd warned them, after seeing them light a fire, that if they did it again, she'd "go after them", he said. But on the Rupert Iverson murder, the interview had drawn a blank and forensics were yet to confirm anything on what had been seized during the search.

Julie remembered seeing the smouldering ashes in the gun emplacement. But she struggled to believe that kids could be responsible for Iris Haggett falling to her death.

She tucked her Clio into a parking space marked *Visitors* inside the gates of Brinstead High School. Her appointment was with the head, identified by a plaque on her door as J. E. Crowder, Executive Headteacher.

"What can I do for you, Detective Sergeant?" The head stood up from her desk and gave Julie a firm handshake. She was fortyish, slightly older than Julie. "Can I get you anything?"

"No thanks, Mrs Crowder, I'm fine."

Julie explained briefly about the Iris Haggett case. "So, you see, it would be helpful if you could let me have the names of any pupils who live in Tideburgh."

"I see." She turned to her computer. "All of them? Not year seven, surely?"

"No. I'm thinking of the older pupils, aged fifteen or sixteen, say," said Julie.

The head turned to her screen. Her fingers rattled on the keyboard. Then she sat back and said, "We have four of them in years ten and eleven who live in Tideburgh. Aged fourteen and fifteen. Are you sure you want Brinstead, and not a sixth-form college?"

"I believe so, from what I've been told," said Julie. "May I have the details?"

The head took a couple more minutes to copy and paste information from her file before getting up and walking to the printer in the corner of her office.

"Here you are." She handed the sheet to Julie. It contained names and addresses.

"Thank you so much. Could you tell me anything about these boys' behaviour?"

"You'll see that one is a girl, actually. In my experience, girls can be just as disruptive in class as boys. It just depends who they hang out with."

"Are you saying that these pupils are disruptive in class?"

"I'd say that Jason Penfold is the ringleader. He's big for his age and lords it over the others. But Gemma Porter is extremely manipulative and has been caught out for blaming others when she gets into trouble. It usually comes down to their family background, we find. Children left to their own devices, not given enough supervision, that sort of thing."

Julie felt Mrs Crowder's eyes coming to rest on her. The head teacher couldn't be aware that Julie was raising her son alone, but her comment had found its mark.

"There are advantages to being a single parent, actually," she said. She hoped she didn't sound too defensive. "It might sound counter-intuitive, but you can actually spend more quality time with your child."

"Oh. Yes, of course," came the reply. "I was talking about discipline. Anyway, is this all you needed?"

Julie took the hint, folded the sheet of paper and got up to leave, holding out her hand.

"Thanks very much, Mrs Crowder. You've been very helpful," she said.

* * *

Julie got back into the Clio and rang the office. Clayton and Bullard were unavailable.

Was it too early to go knocking on doors in Tideburgh? The pupils on her list were at school. Was it worth it anyway? She might find a parent at home. Her growling stomach told her it was lunchtime. She decided that at last she had time to visit her childhood haunts with their half-buried memories, so she headed for Happisburgh. She parked in the car park at the end of Beach Road, where debris, a ramshackle caravan and the remains of an abandoned home bore witness to the earlier struggles of residents who had lost their battle with the sea. She ate a sandwich while looking out at the churning sea from the shelter of the car.

She brushed the crumbs from her trousers, locked the car, and found a path through wheat stubble towards the lighthouse with its three red-and-white bands. She passed a military pillbox standing between the lighthouse and the cliffs and peered inside. It was strewn with litter and empty beer cans.

The lighthouse itself was dramatically backlit by sunlight, which pierced through the dark clouds. Two cottages stood at the base of the tower behind a wall. But where was the lighthouse keeper?

She knocked on the solid door at the bottom of the lighthouse. No answer. She turned towards a white-painted cottage and saw a curtain twitch. Then the front door opened, and an elderly man appeared.

"You looking for something?"

"I was just wondering if I could visit the lighthouse?" said Julie.

"It's closed," he said, rather sharply. He pointed in the direction of the car park. "Can't you read? There's a sign over there explaining that it's run by volunteers these days and they only let people in on open days."

"So you're not the lighthouse keeper . . ."

"There isn't one these days. It's all automatic. Nothing to do with me. Our cottages are privately owned. But nobody seems to realise that," he snapped.

"I'm so sorry to have bothered you." Just as she was wondering whether to take out her warrant card the door slammed shut.

Julie turned back and followed the coastal path in the other direction. It took her past a magnificent gabled mansion set back from the coast, its wings spread out as though embracing the sea. How long would it be until this too was swallowed up by the waves, she wondered. She checked her watch. She still had time to visit the churchyard. She'd always liked looking at gravestones, seeing the local names, which varied from place to place, and noticing the age of those commemorated by wreaths and freshly heaped earth.

On her way there, she was surprised to see some old flagstones on the ground. With a jolt, she realised they were all that remained of the clifftop caravan site where she'd stayed with her parents. Only the rough rectangles bare of grass, and the occasional hydrangea raising a straggly head, were a reminder of the site which had been moved to safety. The place felt spooky, so close to the cliff edge, and she gave an inward shudder.

A few minutes later she pushed open the church gate after following a lane past the white-painted Hill House Inn where she'd read that Arthur Conan Doyle had once been a guest.

She stood contemplating a simple stone in a corner, in memory of four hundred sailors on HMS *Invincible*, which was wrecked on the treacherous sandbanks off Happisburgh in 1801.

At the far edge of the graveyard, where a hedge had been bent horizontal by the prevailing wind, she gazed towards the headland. She could see the silhouettes of more disused gun emplacements on the clifftop across a field, and, in the distance, the ugly installations of the Bacton gas terminal.

Behind her, in the shadow of St Mary's tall tower, were rows of shiny marble stones laid on the grass. Their simplicity was touching. Some had plastic flowers in little vases. Most of them dated from the last ten years. She stood for a moment on the soil in front of one, in memory of a toddler. Julie almost caught her breath. The little girl was the same age as her Caroline had been when she'd died seventeen years ago. The gravestone read: *Marianne Andrews, died aged 18 months, Always in our hearts*. Julie sighed, stirred by her own memories.

She heard the sound of footsteps on the path behind her and turned round.

"Afternoon." It was a man in overalls, holding a builder's trowel. "You've found little Marianne's grave, I see."

"Yes. She was very young, wasn't she?"

"It were only three months ago that she died. Some say that it weren't natural, what happened to her," he said.

"What do you mean?" Julie bridled. "Was she sick?"

"Parents said it was a cot death. But some say it wasn't an accident."

Julie could feel her legs trembling. She needed to sit down.

"Has anyone come forward officially to press charges?" Should she mention that she was a police officer? "You can't just go round accusing people of killing someone without evidence."

"I'm only telling you what's being said around here."

"Are they local, the family?"

"Tideburgh," he replied. He pointed down the road. "Anyway, I'd best get back to my work."

She watched him walk to the tall church tower where he set to filling in cracks at the base of the structure. What if that poor child had died from the same thing as Caroline? Sudden unexplained death in childhood, they'd called it. There was simply no scientific explanation. Then she had a much darker thought. What if her own memory about Caroline's death was faulty?

Always in our hearts. The sudden tragedy had not only caused a rift with her then-husband, who'd deserted her because he couldn't cope, but triggered a severe bout of OCD. She'd consulted a therapist, who had helped her get the condition more or less under control with cognitive behavioural therapy. Her therapist had led her to confront some of the triggers of her compulsions and obsessions before trying to help her cope with the anxiety. But a grisly murder investigation had the power to send her spiralling back into obsessive handwashing, to the point where her hands could be raw with weals.

We all have our demons, she thought. She had her own coping strategy, the multiple checks and handwashing, while Clayton dealt with his anger issues by kicking over the waste-paper basket.

But now, a doubt had been planted in her mind. She made her way back to the car, where she sat, wringing her hands, and staring out across the waves. She couldn't help thinking about the moment when she went into Caroline's room and opened the curtains to find her perfectly healthy toddler in exactly the same position she'd left her the night before, clutching her stuffed penguin.

Was Caroline already stone cold and lifeless when she turned her over to pick her up? Of course she was. How could anyone have suspected her of suffocating her own child?

CHAPTER NINETEEN

Julie rang the doorbell of a nondescript red-brick house among a string of houses tucked behind the village pond.

A painted wooden sign depicting a wave looming over a flintstone cottage was planted beside the pond and announced to visitors they were entering Tideburgh. The reference wasn't lost on Julie.

A Ford Fiesta was parked on the drive. A net curtain twitched before the front door opened a crack. A woman in her thirties was standing in the doorway.

"Yes?"

Julie showed her warrant card and explained that she was investigating the death of Iris Haggett.

"Is that the poor woman they found on the beach?" the woman asked, opening the door. Her hair was tied back in a ponytail and she was wearing a pair of shabby jeans and a T-shirt. "What's it got to do with me, detective?"

"Well, we've heard that she'd had an argument with a gang of—" As soon as she said the word 'gang', the woman's body stiffened.

"Are you saying my boy's in a gang?" she retorted. Julie tried to stop the conversation derailing.

"No, nothing like that, Mrs Penfold. It's just that one of her neighbours said she had a run-in with some boys who were playing in the old military installations by the cliffs, and so I wanted to ask Jason about that."

"Playing in the tunnels? I can't see there's anything wrong with that, can you? When I was a kid we used to go down there too. It's amazing what you can see."

"Really?"

"Yeah, the army was in the tunnels during the war. There's like an underground room where you can see the metal frames where their bunks were. But it's mainly junk. It's quite frightening, actually — you wouldn't want to go by yourself. And you need to be small to shimmy down into the tunnel. But Jason never told me he'd been playing there."

"Does he go out in the evenings?" Julie asked.

"Yes, sure. With his friends. But how am I supposed to know what they get up to?"

"Maybe you could ask him. I'll have to come back to see Jason after school, maybe tomorrow," said Julie. "Will you be in?"

"Yeah, I'll be in. I lost my job, didn't I? And it's not easy to find one round here," came the reply. "But if I hear that Jason has got himself into trouble, I won't be happy about that, I promise you."

* * *

When Julie got back to the nick, Clayton was putting on his jacket.

"What's going on, guv?" she asked.

"I got the call from the hospital. Dad's on palliative care now. I told Bligh that I'm going home for a few days." Clayton always referred to the Lancashire town where his father lived as home.

"OK. I'm sorry to hear that," she said. "Keep in touch, and good luck."

"You too." He picked up his backpack.

Before he turned to go, she asked, "Are we going to get reinforcements while you're away?"

"I told Bligh that you can manage, with help from Bullard. That OK? And she's the SIO on the case, so just follow up with her."

"Of course. Mandy and the rest of the team are working through our list of interviews. We'll be fine," she said. Mandy was a young DC with a sharp mind. But Julie didn't feel as confident as all that.

"And thanks," she added.

"I'll be back soon," he said. "Don't forget you can always ring me."

This is my chance, she realised as she returned to her desk. *An opportunity to shine*. But two things would have to happen: number one, she'd have to be more assertive. More like Clayton, maybe? Not necessarily. He was much readier to bend the rules than she was. And, number two, Ollie would have to step up.

But Julie's conversation in the graveyard was still on her mind. The death of her own daughter must have triggered a rumour mill of suspicion, and that was in the days before 24/7 social media. She googled the name 'Marianne Andrews'. Her search produced a number of hits on local newspapers which reported the 'tragic' death of the toddler without further comment. There was no suggestion of foul play.

But on Twitter, she found #MarianneAndrews in a couple of tweets which had been liked by a dozen people. The Twitter account called itself @justiceformarianne. So the man in the churchyard may have been onto something, she thought. The messages stated that the child had died after the return of the father to the family home after a separation, insinuating that the father had been responsible for the little girl's death. *Whose daughter dies when Dad comes home? #justiceformarianne #marianneandrews.*

Julie frowned. An apparent accusation of murder. Had this been investigated at the time? After all, it was only three months ago and she had no recollection of another suspicious death being reported, particularly a case that seemed to mirror that of her own daughter's. Or was this another sign of the toxic effect of social media poisoning relations in the village? She was about to dive into the police records when her phone rang.

It was Bligh, inviting her up to her office.

"Dennis Iverson has been in here," she said. "He's on the warpath."

Julie got up and went to the window by Clayton's desk, which was cluttered with books. She was just in time to see a Rolls creep out of the car park, under the gaze of a group of curious police officers.

CHAPTER TWENTY

Julie took the stairs up to Bligh's office, wondering whether to voice her concerns about the death of Marianne Andrews.

But she decided against it. *Haven't we got enough pressing things to do?*

Bligh's door was open and she waved her in.

"Do sit down. I mentioned to DI Clayton that we can continue to make progress on this case in his absence without bringing in new team members who'd have to read in. I take it you're fine with temporarily leading the investigation?"

"Yes, of course, ma'am. You said that Mr Iverson has been in?"

"Yes. He wanted us to know that he's filed a complaint about the online abuse and they're looking into it downstairs. He's also extremely disappointed in the lack of progress in the murder investigation. I must say he's taking his feud with the Tideburgh villagers very personally. It sounds like it's reaching boiling point with some of the residents on Blackberry Lane. He seems to think they've got a vendetta against him."

"But enough for one of them to kill his son?" Julie asked.

"That's what remains to be seen," said Bligh. "He mentioned two people in particular, as well as Richard Fairbairn of course. A green activist named Keith Hawkins, who's accused the council of failing to protect the houses on the cliffs. But Iverson said to me that although the council is responsible for defences where there are cliffs, the grant aid and the permissions come from central government. And the problem is that they haven't got any money. So he maintains that although the local authority has the responsibility on paper, in reality they can't do anything with it."

This sounded familiar to Julie from her conversations with Iverson and Fairbairn. Maybe the locals were just turning a deaf ear to reality because they didn't like Iverson.

"Oh, and the other one is a talk radio show host, Alex Howard."

Julie made a note. *Talk radio, this is all we need*, she thought.

"Got it. Dave Bullard and I will be in Tideburgh tomorrow," she said. "But do we have anything more from forensics on Iris Haggett and from the stuff we got from Richard Fairbairn's place? That could be really helpful in determining whether there's a connection to Dennis Iverson."

"I'll let you know as soon as I hear," said Bligh. Julie should have known better than to ask.

"Oh, and one more thing," said Bligh. "Tread carefully tomorrow with those schoolkids. If we're about to charge a fourteen- or fifteen-year-old with attempted murder, we'd better be sure of ourselves."

* * *

It was late afternoon the next day by the time they got going. Julie wanted to make sure that the people they wanted to interview in Tideburgh were going to be in.

"Did you hear about Dennis Iverson coming in yesterday?" Julie asked Bullard, who was seated beside her in the car.

He grinned. "Certainly did. Not only that but I saw his car . . . does he think he's going to impress everyone with his Rolls?"

"He's also got a Tesla." Julie changed the Vauxhall's gears with a jolt.

"Good old Anglian Constabulary," Bullard remarked.

"So the plan is, you do Blackberry Lane, and I'll take the kids and their parents," said Julie.

"Yes, boss," said Bullard. Julie had expected that kind of sarcastic reaction from him, given their unspoken rivalry. But what did he expect? There was an office hierarchy after all, and DS was ahead of DC in the pecking order.

The red-and-white stripes of the Happisburgh lighthouse came into view, and Julie turned onto the road into Tideburgh where she parked in the usual spot near the cliffs at the end of Blackberry Lane.

"I'll meet you back here," she said.

Bullard unstrapped his safety belt. "Are you going to arrest those kids for murder?"

"Depends what their story is," said Julie. "I'm going to see the one described as a ringleader first. A boy named Jason Penfold. His mum knows what's up, so I'll see how that goes. I want to get to the bottom of what the hell they were doing in those tunnels that attracted Iris Haggett's attention."

She watched Bullard's tall figure, capped by a blond tousle, head towards Blackberry Lane on foot. She walked the few yards to Iris Haggett's property where she stood and looked eastwards towards the gun emplacement. She calculated it would be a ten-minute walk at most to get there. If Haggett had been sitting outside, or even looked through a window, she would have seen the glow of a fire before setting out to remonstrate with the youths. But what could have caused her to fall to her death after dark?

She got back into the car. A few minutes later, she was ringing the doorbell at Mrs Penfold's house.

The door opened straight away. "Hello, sergeant. I've been expecting you."

Julie went in and was led into a sitting room where a sullen-looking boy was sitting in an armchair studying his phone. His long legs were stretched out in front of him, in the direction of the TV.

"You must be Jason," she said. He grunted. Julie looked across at his mother, who was standing with her arms folded. The slightly sickening smell of fried food drifted into the room from the kitchen.

"Now, Jason. Tell the detective what you told me about what you were doing in the tunnel the other night." Mrs Penfold seemed to be angry. "Jason. Come on," she repeated.

The boy mumbled something in a low voice and put his phone on his lap.

"Excuse me?" said Julie. "Jason, we just need to know what happened when Iris Haggett came over to complain to you and your friends."

"She saw the lights," he said.

"Wait a minute. Are we talking about the same night? Do you mean she came over and complained about you lighting a fire?"

"No. That was before. She came back three or four days ago when we were messing about with a couple of laser pens."

"Laser pens?"

"Yes." His mother was shaking her head. "They bought them online. I gave Jason a laser tag game for his birthday, you see, and they played in the garden with it."

"Laser tag?" said Julie. "I didn't realise you could play that at home."

"Oh yes. We went once to a place in Norwich and Jason and his friends loved it. So this game means they can play as long as they like without me having to book it and drive them there. I didn't mind if they took the game into the field — it says it's infrared so it can't harm you. But I didn't know that after that they'd gone and bought laser pointers, did I, Jason?" She stared at him as though demanding a confession.

"Is that right, Jason?" asked Julie. She remembered newspaper accounts of how pilots landing or taking off from airports had been temporarily blinded by laser rays. Is this what had happened to Iris Haggett?

Jason nodded slowly, his eyes narrowed.

"So tell me what happened," said Julie, sitting down. "How many of you were there that night?"

"Just the three of us. Me, Gemma Porter and Johnny Gates," he said. "The woman must have seen the green rays from the pens. They were great — we were pointing them into the sky. She came over shouting at us, saying they could crash a plane or something. We didn't realise that they were so powerful, honest."

Julie, perched on the edge of her seat, recognised the two other names from the list she'd been given at the school. She waited for Jason to carry on.

He looked up at his mother before continuing. "So anyway, we were playing, weren't we, and we might have pointed one of them in her direction, and then she started screaming and running in circles before she ran off."

"Who might have pointed it in her direction? Who was holding the pens?" Julie asked.

"I don't remember at that moment who was. We had two pens and there were three of us. But we all tried them. Like I say, it was fun."

Julie frowned. She wondered whether he'd been coached by his mother to play down his role. "Did you see her run off the cliff?"

"It was dark, wasn't it? We thought she'd run home. The next thing I knew was when I heard they'd found a body on the beach but I didn't realise straightaway that it was her."

"Did you think she might have been temporarily blinded?"

"Not straightaway, no. Then I googled it and saw that's what might have happened. I was going to say something, but I didn't know how. I thought it might go away."

"What about the others?" Julie said.

"They agreed with me," said Jason. He was staring at Julie as though relieved to have got this off his chest.

Mrs Penfold was still standing with her arms folded. "So what happens now, sergeant? He says he was going to say something, so that must count in his favour, surely?"

"I'm going to ask you both to come back to the police station with me," she said.

"But my Jason's only fifteen," Mrs Penfold protested. "He's a child. They didn't mean no harm."

"Yes, I'm aware of that. His case will be dealt with by the youth courts in the first instance, for that reason," said Julie. "But we'll need to interview Jason's two other friends as well."

Julie took them outside and opened the car door for Mrs Penfold and her son to get into the back.

Bullard was waiting for them in the car park, watching the waves crash onto the beach.

"Everything OK?" Bullard asked Julie quietly as he shut his door.

She nodded. "We've got three teenage suspects here. But which of them is responsible? Jason's trying to muddy the waters. Better make sure that we get the others in as soon as possible."

CHAPTER TWENTY-ONE

Julie sensed a presence behind her as she hunched over her computer, writing up her notes.

She knew from the throat-clearing that it was Bligh who was her morning visitor.

"Well done on the Iris Haggett case," Julie heard her say. She turned round and saw that Bligh was smiling.

"Ma'am?"

"At last we've got some good news, although not yet for the Iverson case. This laser pen theory is very interesting. It shows there was no connection between the two deaths in Tideburgh."

"Yes, but we still need to find out exactly what happened. The three kids have had time to get their stories straight so it'll be hard to discover which one targeted Iris Haggett."

"I'm waiting to hear from forensics about possible damage to the woman's retina. That would confirm whether she fell to her death because she couldn't see where she was going. Dreadful." She turned to go. "Let me know how it goes with the three adolescents. You'll be interviewing them separately?"

"Yes. With their parents."

"Tricky," said Bligh, and walked off.

As soon as Bligh had left the detective suite, Bullard appeared at Julie's side as if by magic.

"What did she want?" he asked. He drew up a chair.

"Oh, it was about the Iris Haggett case. How did you get on yesterday down Blackberry Lane? I've not had time to read your report yet."

"They're certainly worked up about the council. And Iverson in particular, because he's the elected member with the coastal management portfolio. They've heard that there's no scheme available for the people whose homes are at risk, like they had in Happisburgh a few years ago. So they feel their homes are being sacrificed to the waves."

"I can imagine how I'd feel," said Julie. "But didn't you say the guy you saw is a green activist? Could there be a political aspect to the row with Iverson?"

"I don't think so. The majority of council members are Lib Dem, and Dennis Iverson's an independent. So it's not like a fight you might have between Labour and Tories."

"OK."

"So this guy Keith Hawkins sat me down and showed me maps. He really knows his stuff," said Bullard. "He explained that the government is responsible for sea defences, and the council for coastal protection where there are cliffs. He says that they should never have allowed concrete sea defences to be built further up the coast. That's what they say had a counterproductive effect down the coast in Tideburgh."

"And what else?"

"That's it, really. The main thing is what I said about the precedent in Happisburgh. The Tideburgh villagers don't understand why the council can't persuade the government to do a deal like last time."

"Oh, Iverson told me all about that. About that being a pilot scheme and that's why there's no more money. Didn't you read what I filed on the system about this before seeing Hawkins?"

"I can't say I did. Sorry."

"Dave, if you can't keep up we're going to keep going round in circles," she retorted.

He seemed surprised by her tone of voice.

"Anything else?"

Bullard took out his notebook and flicked through the pages. "It's flaring up like a hornet's nest now, thanks to what happened to Iris Haggett."

"What do you mean?" she asked.

"They're worried about the council putting pressure on the other residents of Blackberry Lane to move out. They seem to think that it's suspicious that she died because she was refusing to leave her property. Richard Fairbairn is seen as the obvious next victim. In fact, one woman I spoke to on Blackberry Lane was convinced that Dennis Iverson was behind Iris Haggett's death. To get her out of the way, you know."

"Get her out of the way for what?" said Julie. "Good grief, you mean that they think Dennis Iverson wants to kill Richard Fairbairn? These villagers are conspiracy theorists! What on earth would Dennis Iverson or the council gain from killing people whose houses are about to fall into the sea? They're worthless! Do you know what I think? I reckon these villagers hate him because he's a builder and they see him as profiting from their misery."

"Oh. I hadn't thought about that." He stretched out his legs, sucking his pen. Then he flicked through more pages of his notebook.

"Here we are. You could be right," he conceded. "But what's interesting is that it isn't just about the houses that are falling down, apparently. Hawkins told me that one of the houses on Blackberry Lane has just been sold. And guess who is going to build a new one for the seller?"

"Don't tell me . . . Dennis Iverson!" said Julie. She remembered what Richard Fairbairn had told her about how one or two of the Blackberry Lane residents had been able to sell, despite the environmental risks to their property.

"Very interesting," she said.

Bullard nodded. "Again, according to Hawkins, Iverson's going to do a deal with a developer who's talking to a local farmer about a plot."

"Right. But they'd still need planning permission . . ." said Julie. "This reminds me of what Iverson told me about a building project in Tideburgh years ago when he was on the council planning team. He says that's what one of the Facebook messages accusing him of corruption is about. But he insists everything was above board."

"OK. Maybe that's what they're talking about. Of course. He had to stand down for the vote on the plans laid out by the committee officer, right? But after everyone voted in favour of the developer's application, again according to Hawkins, the villagers are convinced that Dennis Iverson lobbied some of the committee members to get their approval!"

"And now, they suspect he's going to do it again . . . but is it true?"

"It's easy enough to find out, boss. The council meetings are recorded."

"I'll get Mandy to check this out," said Julie. She'd just about had enough of Bullard.

"And what about the talk-show host? What did he have to say for himself?" she went on.

"Oh, I didn't have time," he said.

CHAPTER TWENTY-TWO

Julie swallowed her irritation and rang the talk-show host on his mobile as soon as Bullard was out of sight. The signal was so poor that he returned her call on his landline.

When she asked about relations with Dennis Iverson, Alex Howard told her that he'd devoted a show to coastal erosion in Tideburgh in August. But the expert being interviewed on the show was soon drowned out by villagers calling in to complain about Dennis Iverson's role on the council.

"One of them got so worked up I had to shut him down before he made a fool of himself," he said. "The air in the studio was turning blue."

"Could you send me a link to that particular show?" Julie asked.

"With pleasure," he responded.

* * *

A little later, Julie and Bullard were called downstairs, where Jason Penfold was waiting with his mother. He was the first of the Brinstead High pupils to be interviewed under caution on suspicion of manslaughter.

He'd lost the bravado of the day before and seemed overawed by the bare interview room. He sat hunched over the table, his mother sitting erect next to him. His hair was combed flat for the occasion. When Julie asked him if he understood the terms of the caution, he replied in a low voice.

But still, he stuck to the line that he'd given Julie the day before: an admission to having played with the laser pens at the gun emplacement, and to having been the target of Iris Haggett's tongue. But he repeated that he was unable to recall who exactly had held the pen that may have temporarily blinded her and led to her death.

Julie and Bullard suggested a break after less than an hour. The boy and his mother were taken to see the custody officer, who would let him go home on bail. They'd gone at it from every angle but hadn't broken down Jason's line of defence.

"This is annoying," Julie said to Bullard outside in the corridor. "If all three of them say the same thing, what can we do?"

"Let's see what Bligh says, after we've interviewed the other two. I expect she'll ask the CPS to approve manslaughter charges. And the techies might find fingerprints on the laser pens, right?"

"Yes. But what if all their fingerprints are on both of the pens?" said Julie. "And of course they were completely off the grid. Not only was it pitch dark, but there was no CCTV out there on the headland, obviously."

They went back inside where Gemma Porter and her father were waiting for them. The girl's fingernails were bitten to the quick but her eyes, rimmed with dark eyeliner, were defiant. Julie remembered that the head teacher at the school had said she was manipulative.

They went through her details. She looked older than her given age of fifteen because of the make-up. It didn't escape Julie's notice that she was only a few years older than Ollie. She read her the caution and asked if she understood. Gemma nodded.

"Could you speak up please, Gemma? This is being recorded," Julie said gently.

"Yes," came the reply. There was a touch of insolence in the girl's voice. The father, dressed in a suit and with a face like a ferret, gave her a sharp look.

"Tell us about the first time Iris Haggett came across the field to tell you off at the gun emplacement," said Julie.

"Not much to say, really," said Gemma.

"What was the reason she came over?"

"It was a cold night, and we'd set a couple of twigs on fire to keep warm."

"A couple of twigs? I was there the next day and I can tell you it was more than a couple of twigs. The ashes were still warm."

Gemma looked at her in surprise. "Well, anyway, we set a fire," she said. "And the woman—"

"Iris Haggett."

"She accused us of, I don't know, dangerous behaviour, something like that. But there was no danger to anybody."

"Did she say anything else?" Bullard asked.

"She said we could've set the field on fire, that sort of thing. She was probably worried about her house."

"So you knew where she lived?" Julie asked.

"Everyone knows the two of them, the ones at the end of Blackberry Lane," came the reply. "They're weirdos."

"Weirdos? Why do you say that?" Julie asked.

Gemma shrugged. She looked down at her chewed fingernails before replying, "Just saying. She was hysterical when she came running over to complain about our little fire."

"And the next time you saw her was when, exactly? Two or three nights later?"

"Two nights later, yes."

Julie continued the questioning. "You recognised her when she came across the field, did you?"

"It was dark. But we recognised her voice, yeah."

"What was the reason for her complaint that night?" said Bullard.

"She saw we were playing with the lasers. She must've seen the green lights in the sky."

"How many lasers did you have?"

"We got two."

"So you were sharing them, were you?" Julie asked.

"That's right."

"And then what happened? How close did she get?"

"Not very close. She was shouting at us, wasn't she? One of the others grabbed the laser from me and shone it towards her. That's when she went back."

Julie bit down her frustration. "Who grabbed the laser from you? Jason or Johnny?" .

"One of them. I can't remember," said Gemma. Julie and Bullard exchanged a look.

"And then what?"

"Jason and Johnny fist-bumped," said Gemma, matter-of-factly.

"Why did they do that?"

Gemma shrugged. "Because she'd gone away."

"So did you see where she went?"

"I told you. It was dark. We thought she'd gone home, didn't we?"

Bullard stepped in. "When you say that you knew where Iris Haggett lived, had she complained to you on other occasions, earlier?"

"In the summer, yeah. She'd call out to us, rude things, like, 'Ain't you got no homes to go to?' when she'd see us out by the tunnel. But we weren't doing anything wrong, just playing," the girl said, with a sideways look at her father.

"And when you heard that Iris Haggett had been found dead, what did you think?" Julie asked.

"Nothing, why?"

"So you didn't think it might have had something to do with you?" said Julie, leaning across the table.

Gemma shrugged again. "No, of course not."

They wound up the interview and the pair were sent to see the custody officer about bail for Gemma.

"Jesus Christ, a fist bump!" said Julie, as soon as the girl and her father were out of earshot. "They celebrated getting rid of her. They must have known they'd lasered her in the eyes."

"But can we prove it?" asked Bullard.

CHAPTER TWENTY-THREE

Johnny Gates was sitting at the table in the interview room, next to a young man in a pullover and jeans.

"Excuse me," the man said, standing up as soon as Julie and Bullard walked in. "How long is this going to take?"

"Are you Mr Gates — Johnny's father?" Julie asked. He nodded. "It won't take long. We just need Johnny's account of what happened at the tunnels the other night. You'll be aware that we're investigating the death of Iris Haggett."

"Yes," he said, looking at his son whose eyes were riveted to the table. "But I have to get back to the farm before it gets dark. It's a busy time at the moment." Julie noticed dirt under the fingernails of his hands, which were strong and weather-beaten.

"Of course. Let's get your details first." Johnny seemed unsettled when she read out the caution, and again she wondered whether the three pupils had agreed a version of what happened that night.

"Come on, Johnny," she urged. "What do you remember about the night that Iris Haggett came over to tell you off? What were you doing, the three of you?"

"Which time?" he asked.

"Let's start with the first time."

"Well, the first time we were playing underground, and she shouted down the manhole and told us we shouldn't be down there," he said.

"How did she know you were there?"

"She must've seen us on the cliff path. It was still daylight then."

"How long ago was this?"

"About a month ago. She had it in for us, all right. Then when we lit a fire another time she came over 'specially to complain. And the third time was the other night when we were shooting lasers into the sky."

"How close did she get to you that evening?" Bullard asked.

"I don't know. It was dark, see. We could hear her but couldn't see who it was exactly."

"But one of you turned their laser on her. Who was it?" Bullard continued.

Johnny looked at his father. Then he said, "Gemma."

"Are you sure?" Julie asked.

"Yeah," came the reply.

"And what about two of you doing a fist bump after the light was shone at Iris Haggett?" Bullard asked. Johnny looked genuinely puzzled.

"Fist bump? I don't know nothing about no fist bump," he said. "We went back to playing with the lasers after she went away."

* * *

Julie stood outside the interview room shaking her head.

"That was fun," she said. "Three kids with three different stories. And now they're all going home on bail."

"Yes." Bullard ran his fingers through his thick blond hair. "But it certainly sounds like the woman had it in for them."

"But maybe she was right? It was dangerous, what they were doing. Goodness knows what could have happened to them down in that tunnel."

She felt Bullard was judging her for being prim and proper but before she could say more, a message arrived on her phone from Bligh.

"Bligh's talking to the CPS about manslaughter charges," she told Bullard. "And then it's out of our hands. The youth court can decide what to do about them."

"Do you fancy a cuppa?" Bullard asked.

"Have you got time to dip into the talk radio show about Tideburgh? I can set it up here if you can bring the teas up."

"Yes, boss," he said. His tone of voice said everything.

By the time Bullard returned, Julie had set up her computer with two sets of earphones.

"Be my guest," she said, gesturing to the chair next to hers.

The show started off with an alarming description of the environmental damage to the Norfolk coastline, by the expert introduced as Professor George Mackintosh. He predicted an accelerating pace of coastal erosion driven by climate change. He went on to warn that Tideburgh was particularly affected because of the cliffs made up of boulder clay which collapses when wet. So far, so familiar.

But the floodgates opened when Howard invited callers' questions. They were soon attacking the council, and the coastal management committee in particular. A caller who identified himself as 'Mike' began a long rant. "Don't you realise we can't go on like this," he concluded. "We have to do something to save our community. In the past twenty years, do you know how many houses and businesses we've lost?"

"Yes, I am aware. But we have to face up to reality. We can't save every home from the sea," said the professor. "I should point out that the village got its name originally from the tides, although the local pronunciation corrupted the meaning over time. And the North Sea has been eroding the coast for the past five thousand years. In fact, you may not be aware of this, but Tideburgh church fell into the sea a few centuries ago."

Julie had wondered why there was a Vicarage Road in Tideburgh. Now she knew why it no longer led to the church.

But the callers didn't want to dwell on local history. Mackintosh's remark brought a new surge of questions from listeners accusing the district council of failing to protect the cliffside homes sufficiently. Mackintosh patiently explained the background about how it took time to agree financial mechanisms with the central government that could help those at risk.

"There's a great injustice here," he said. "At present, residents living on the coast can lose everything, through no fault of their own, and they're not entitled to anything from anyone. But it's not the fault of the council. It's government policy that's to blame."

The government had concluded that building new coastal defences couldn't be justified after a cost-benefit analysis, he said.

"So we're buggered, then?" said Howard.

"Indeed you are," the professor replied. "Right now, there's no long-term plan, unfortunately." He paused for a moment, before adding, "It's tragic, really, because it's our coastal heritage which is gradually disappearing."

"What about Dennis Iverson?" said a caller named Jenny. "He's the coastal management committee chairman but he doesn't even live here! He rents out his mansion in Tideburgh for parties and gay orgies!"

"As Mr Iverson isn't present to defend himself, I think we'd better steer clear of personal insults," Howard interjected.

After about twenty minutes of the hour-long show, Julie stopped the recording and took off her earphones.

"Heard enough?" she said. "I don't think we're going to learn anything more here, are we? We already know that this village on the edge of England is having a collective nervous breakdown."

"Yes, we already got the picture." Bullard sipped his tea.

"Bottom line is they all hate Dennis Iverson and somehow blame him for their predicament. But is it possible that one of them hates him so much that they killed his son? And if so, who was it?"

CHAPTER TWENTY-FOUR

Once Bullard had gone, Julie realised she had an opportunity to look into the case of the dead child whose grave she'd seen in Tideburgh. She began digging into the coroners' records and quickly found the name of Marianne Andrews.

The cause of death was stated as sudden unexplained death in childhood, or SUDC. There it was. The same tragedy that had killed Caroline. Julie's heart went out to the parents. But she wanted to know more. She wondered whether she could justify calling the pathologist on the case, Dr Jennifer Cooper, without raising suspicion. Before she realised what she was doing, she was calling Cooper's number.

When the pathologist picked up, Julie wasted no time in explaining what she'd been told at the graveside of Marianne Andrews.

"So, excuse me, but before I take this any further, I'm wondering whether you might have had any suspicions yourself that it might have been something other than SUDC?" Julie asked. "In terms of possible parental abuse?"

"I remember that case well," the pathologist said. "The cot deaths that I've had to deal with have been of babies, not toddlers like this one. I think that's probably even tougher for the parents to handle, because their child is beginning to walk and talk, and they wouldn't be concerned about sleep issues. But I didn't have any concerns about this unexplained death, no. Had I done so, I would have reported it to the coroner."

Of course she would.

"I'm sorry I've wasted your time," said Julie, ringing off. She was beginning to wonder if she'd made the call simply to assuage her own conscience about Caroline's death. But surely she was right to follow up on what the man in the churchyard had said. Now she felt she could dismiss it as malicious gossip.

She drove home, where she found Ollie in his usual place in front of his computer upstairs, headphones clamped on his ears. She positioned herself beside him so that he looked up and freed up one ear.

"Take those off, please, Ollie. I've something to say to you."

He took off the headphones.

"Look, there are going to be some changes round here. I've been given more responsibility and it means I'll be spending more time at work on an investigation."

He looked crestfallen.

"It's only for a week or so. Promise," she said. That produced a more positive response.

"But what's that got to do with me?"

"It means that you'll have to do more stuff around the house. Washing up, tidying your bedroom —" she surveyed the piles of clothes on the floor as she spoke — "and even help with the cooking. It wouldn't kill you to peel a potato, you know."

"OK," he said. "Is that it?" He'd turned back to his game before she'd even had time to reply.

"And don't forget to do your homework!" she added in a loud voice.

Sometimes she wondered whether she'd done the right thing, when moving to Norwich, to rent a soulless new house on a suburban estate. But she had to admit it was convenient for work, the shops and Ollie's school. She went into the kitchen where she found herself scrubbing her hands as though her life depended on it. The intrusive thought, *If I don't do this, something terrible will happen to Ollie,* had kicked in again. She was powerless to stop it.

She switched on the oven to heat up ready meals for the two of them and sat down in front of the TV. The local news was on. The top story was about a homophobic attack in Norwich outside a gay pub. The victim had been attacked at eleven o'clock the night before when leaving a pub with a couple of friends. They showed a picture of the man, his face swollen and bruised. She didn't recognise him, but she recognised the name. Julie's hand flew to her mouth. It was James Crofton, the estate agent who'd gone to the party in drag as Henriette. The report didn't mention the party, but did say that it came after Rupert Iverson, the son of local builder, Dennis Iverson, had been found dead after an apparent homophobic attack.

'*An apparent homophobic attack*.' There it was again, the baseless speculation about Rupert being gay. And why homophobic? Describing Rupert's death as an apparent homophobic attack could imply that the killer came from outside the party circle. *What are we missing here?*

Julie stared at the TV. Had Jonathan Murray found out about Brian's relationship with James? And possibly that he'd been at the party disguised as Henriette, the woman whose death was shrouded in mystery?

Who was the suspect in the poisoning of Henriette? It was the Chevalier de Lorraine, she remembered. And Jonathan Murray had gone to the party in that role.

How strange it was that the parallel narrative from the court of Versailles might still be playing out on a cobbled street in Norwich, even after Rupert's death.

CHAPTER TWENTY-FIVE

Bligh was waiting for them all to assemble in the incident room. The board behind her was a jumble of photos and names.

"Morning, all. We're making good progress here. Certainly we've now established that there was no connection between the murders of Rupert Iverson and Iris Haggett." She paused to indicate the two on the wall behind her, which were displayed separately. "Indeed we have three suspects, all minors, in the Haggett case, who are believed to have temporarily blinded her while playing with laser pens at a gun emplacement near to her home."

Bligh glanced towards the press officer who was on the front row. "As some of you are aware, I'll be holding a press conference shortly. The youngsters, aged fourteen and fifteen, are going to be charged with manslaughter. Let's hope that the ringleader can be flushed out."

She went on, "Now, we also have a series of interesting findings from forensics. First of all, they confirm that Iris Haggett's retinas were damaged in both eyes. So that does point to the laser pen being shone in her direction. Now from what we've heard, I don't believe the youngsters intended to kill her, but it would explain how she fell to her death."

She turned back to the board and gestured towards the section featuring the Rupert Iverson murder.

"I must say that until now, we've been making slow progress on the Iverson murder. It looked like a closed-circle mystery at first, but frankly this is Agatha Christie on steroids."

Julie exchanged a grim smile with Bullard.

"We may have a breakthrough thanks to forensics, who have established that Rupert Iverson's DNA is on the handle of an outdoor broom taken from Richard Fairbairn's house."

Everyone was hanging on her words. This was quite a surprise.

"It's been scrubbed, but there is touch DNA from Richard Fairbairn and from another unidentified person on the handle. It's possible that this was the murder weapon. However Fairbairn's DNA is not on the cricket bat found on the beach. There is touch DNA from more than one unidentified person on the bat. I suppose that's not surprising as it was used in a cricket match on the afternoon of the party. But this is good progress."

Bligh continued, "Secondly, Rupert Iverson's DNA has been identified from a semen stain on the billiards table. Now, the most obvious explanation is that he hooked up with someone there, either during the party or afterwards — perhaps that's why he left the bedroom. But it would be helpful if we could obtain an explanation. Any questions so far?"

Nobody spoke. Bligh looked at Julie and added, "I want you to check out the broom and Richard Fairbairn's account. In the next few days we'll have to go through the entire guest list again to make sure we have DNA samples from all the guests, which will help us to eliminate suspects."

She waited while the assembled officers digested the information before saying, "According to the forensic analysis, as we suspected, there are signs of a struggle in the summer house. It's extremely likely that's where Rupert was attacked before he was taken to the pool. We have plenty of prints from the wine bottles. In my mind, that could point to the murderer, or murderers, being among the guests. That's why we need to analyse all their samples urgently."

Bligh ended the meeting and everyone shuffled out. Bullard said to Julie, "Well, at least Rupert had a shag before he died."

Julie sighed. "Who's your money on? My bet's on Bethany. I'll approach her. Do you want to check with Cathy? It's a bit awkward because she told me that she didn't know why the billiards room was in such a mess."

"I wonder if she was telling the truth."

Julie noticed that Bligh was still in the room, picking up a file.

"Ma'am?" she said.

Bligh put her file down. "Everything all right? Can you arrange for Richard Fairbairn to come in?"

"Yes, no problem. I just wanted to ask you, though, whether you'd seen that one of Rupert's party guests was attacked in a homophobic incident in Norwich? It was on the news last night. The reporter said it came after Rupert died in an apparently homophobic attack."

"What? Where on earth has that come from? I'll have a word with the press officer."

"I was thinking, as well, that his parents would be upset to think that this is where the investigation has led us. His father was quite angry when we asked about his sexuality — he seemed quite sensitive about it."

"Good grief," said Bligh. "But wait a minute . . . was Rupert bisexual? Do you think there might be a crime-of-passion angle? Someone we haven't looked at as a suspect?"

Julie hesitated. "Everyone we've spoken to is adamant that he was straight. I really don't see this as an angle in this investigation."

"Agreed. I'll make this quite clear when I speak to the media."

"The thing is, though, ma'am, you just mentioned that you think it was someone from among the guests. But what about the assumption that it was someone from outside the circle who wanted to hurt Rupert's father by targeting the son? Because that's why we've been focusing on the villagers, and people like Richard Fairbairn with an axe to grind," Julie ventured. "Or are we wrong?"

"At this stage, given what we now have from forensics, I don't think we can rule anything out. The DNA implicating Richard Fairbairn is intriguing," said Bligh. "And there could be a reason that the journalists are referring to a homophobic attack. Sometimes they have sources that we don't know about. Or they might just be jumping to conclusions."

* * *

Julie went downstairs to her desk. Where had this story come from? Was it that story from the gossip site being recycled all over again? Had a reporter talked to the villagers who'd watched the cricket match? But that wouldn't have told them the partygoers were gay, only that one of the men had been dressed as a woman, and in a costume which was clearly fancy dress. Or maybe it was simply wild speculation based on the debauchery portrayed in *Versailles*. Everyone in Norfolk must by now be aware of the inspiration for Rupert's party.

She dug out Terry Monahan's mobile number and he picked up straight away.

"Was Rupert gay?" he said, repeating her question. "Not since school, as far as I know," he added with a laugh.

She was struck by his answer. "I'm just wondering whether you've been contacted by any reporters since Rupert died."

"Yes I was, as a matter of fact. They wanted to know about his relationships. I didn't mention Bethany. Rupert wanted it to be a secret."

"Thank you. But you might have said something about his school days?"

"Possibly. I don't recall," said Monahan. "I did talk about the party, of course. It was called 'In the court of the Sun King', remember?"

"And about Brian Mason in drag?"

Monahan laughed. "The journalist already knew that Brian and Rupert were friends."

"And what about James Crofton? I'm aware that you took a picture of him in costume at the party."

"Oh, yes, James. I did, yes. But I didn't mention him to the reporter. He wasn't in Rupert's inner circle. Did you see he was attacked in Norwich? Terrible."

Julie rang off. Could journalists have got hold of the guest list with its clues? The thought made her nervous. But she had the original with its crossings-out, didn't she?

She reported back to Bligh that the press reports had no firm basis and had probably been built around an innuendo from Terry Monahan.

She was collecting her things together when the office phone rang. It was a voice with a familiar northern accent.

"Hello, Sam. How's it going up there? How's your dad?"

"That's why I'm ringing. He died the day before yesterday."

"Oh, I'm so sorry."

"Yeah." Clayton sounded upset. But he ploughed on. "I'll have to stay up here for a few more days. I'm organising the funeral and all."

"Of course. Did you talk to the boss?"

"Yes, I just spoke to her."

"Where are you staying?"

"I'm at my dad's place in Garstang. It's all very weird. It's strange not to have him around, and to be here on my own. Friends of his keep showing up to pay their respects and I haven't a clue who they are . . . Anyway, how's the Iverson case going?"

Julie wondered whether she should broach the issue on her mind. Clayton had enough to worry about, after all.

"Well, there's been an attack on James Crofton, remember him?"

"You mean the one in the frock?" *Was he winding her up*?

"Yes. One of Rupert's gay friends who was at the party. He was injured in Norwich last night. And the media are saying that Rupert himself may have been killed in a homophobic attack. It's annoying because we've no idea where they've got that from. We're about to interview Richard Fairbairn about why a broom at his place has got Rupert's DNA on it."

"You mean he was involved in the attack?"

"That's what we're trying to find out," she said.

"Do you want me to find out where this story about Rupert came from? I could make a call or two."

Julie knew exactly who he was referring to. "Don't worry, Sam, honestly. You've got enough to do. We'll keep plugging away here. And we're finding plenty more villagers with a grudge against Dennis Iverson."

Clayton didn't respond immediately. She imagined that his mind must be elsewhere. Maybe the media were making it up.

"Look, I'll let you get on with your stuff. Keep in touch," she said.

CHAPTER TWENTY-SIX

Richard Fairbairn was brought in the next morning by a DC who'd been sent to pick him up from his home. Luckily he was in when she called.

He'd requested a duty solicitor on his way to the nick. Now, he sat across from Julie and Bullard in an interview room, accompanied by a young solicitor. He must have realised that being questioned a second time, this time under caution, could have consequences.

Julie switched on the tape. She wondered whether Bligh would be monitoring the interview upstairs.

Richard, who'd given his age as fifty-nine, looked uncomfortable on the chair which seemed too small for his bulk.

Julie kicked off the interview by saying, "I must inform you that we've found Rupert Iverson's fingerprints on the broom handle that was taken by our forensics department from your home."

He looked at her as though to say, *So what?* But apparently thought better of speaking the words aloud.

"We believe that it may have been used to attack Rupert Iverson," Julie continued.

"And you're saying that this has something to do with me?" Richard said loudly. "How long is this going to take? I've left my dog at home."

"I'm asking you if this is your broom?"

"It is now," he said. "I found it on the beach a couple of weeks ago."

Bullard and Julie exchanged a look.

"You're going to tell us exactly when you found it, Mr Fairbairn. This is a matter of the utmost importance."

He leaned back in the chair, frowning.

"I can't remember exactly," he said, looking at the solicitor for support.

"OK. Well, if I may refresh your memory, the broom was on your property when I came to interview you about Iris Haggett," Julie said.

"Ah, yes. Right." That seemed to have jogged his memory. "I remember when the police came round after the Iverson murder with all the tape that they put round the field. It was definitely after that. Yes," he said firmly.

"So you're saying that you found the brush on the beach after Rupert Iverson was murdered?" said Bullard.

"That's right. Definitely."

"And what exactly were you doing on the beach when you found it?"

"Beachcombing, wasn't I? You can pick up all sorts of stuff lying around, sometimes washed up by the waves. Usually it's just driftwood. I collect it. I was walking the dog and I found the broom at the bottom of the cliff, as though someone had thrown it away." Richard suddenly realised what he had said. "Oh. You mean that the person who murdered Rupert Iverson threw away the weapon and I picked it up?"

"When you say it was at the bottom of the cliff, please tell us the exact location."

"You know where the road kind of stops dead? It was on the beach below that," he replied. "We went down from my place, down the path by the car park onto the beach and then along in the direction of Happisburgh. I hadn't gone very far when I saw it."

"And you didn't think of mentioning it to anyone?"

"Why would I? I didn't know it was used as a murder weapon until you said so just now!" he insisted.

"Is there any reason why you would have washed the handle?"

He seemed surprised by the question. "Washed it? I always clean what I pick up from the beach. It was grubby and I didn't know how long it had been there, did I?"

"Mr Fairbairn, thank you very much, that's all for now." Julie switched off the tape.

"Christ, it's just as well we didn't arrest him," said Bullard, when he'd gone. "Do you believe him?"

"Yes, I do," said Julie. "He doesn't seem like a barefaced liar to me. And he was the one who helped us by saying that Iris Haggett had gone after those kids. What do you think?"

"I agree."

"This case is falling apart. Our only hope now is that forensics can come through on the other prints on the brush. But at least now we know what happened. The murderer, or murderers, took the broom and threw it over the cliff, presumably thinking that the tide would carry it away."

"So now it looks like there were two people, one wielding the cricket bat and the other with the broom. Both of which were in the summer house."

* * *

Bligh was expecting them, and beckoned them in.

They talked through the likely suspects one more time, from party guests to a villager with a grudge. The very same suspects since day one.

"So where does this leave us?" Bligh asked. "Does it seem to you that Rupert's relationship with Bethany Price is a key issue?"

Julie shook her head. "It seemed like it might be at first, but I think we've ruled that out now," she said. "Bethany did confirm to me that she and Rupert had sex in the billiards room. Did her boyfriend catch them in the act and kill

Rupert in a jealous rage? We had him in here and, frankly, his alibi stands up."

"Very well. I'm not going to get into these ridiculous press reports about the murder being homophobic because I've already dismissed that theory," said Bligh. She wrote something in her notebook. "What about Dennis Iverson?"

Julie pulled a face. "You mean, did he do it?"

"No. Of course not. Why would he? But what's he got to say for himself with all these villagers up in arms against him?"

Julie felt lame. "Well, we have him down on our list, but since he came in the other day we've not gone back to him. We're trying to finish interviewing everyone from the party, in case someone's memory has been triggered. It's pretty labour-intensive. And we're still collecting their DNA." It sounded like the excuse it was.

"We're on it, ma'am," said Bullard.

Julie felt herself shrink inside. Of course that's what she should have said. That's what Bligh would want to hear. "But is our hypothesis about the murderer wanting to hurt Dennis Iverson by killing his son too complicated? It could just be someone who hated Rupert and used the party as an excuse . . ." Julie's voice trailed off.

"A family member is always most likely," agreed Bligh. "We're sure they've been ruled out?"

"Mrs Iverson is in a wheelchair with MS. She vouches for Jeremy, Rupert's older brother, who says he was at home with her on the night of the party."

Bullard added, "Jeremy is the first to admit the two brothers weren't close, but that's not a crime . . . and according to him, he's well placed to take over the Iverson business, so why would he want to hurt his father?"

"Quite." Something on her computer screen had attracted Bligh's attention. "You'll have heard that Sam's father died?"

"Yes, ma'am," said Julie. "Sad news."

"We'll be sending a wreath from the station, of course." It was a dismissal.

"Do you want to take care of Dennis Iverson and fix up an appointment with him?" Julie asked Bullard as they went down the stairs. "After all, you talked to the residents on Blackberry Lane. I'll check with Mandy about how she's doing with finishing up the interviews. We need to step on the gas at this point."

"Sure," he said.

Julie returned to her desk with a sinking feeling that she wasn't up to the job. Bligh had the uncanny ability to shine a light on your weak spot, even before you'd identified it yourself. Julie sat resting her head in her hands, staring at the empty screen for a while. She'd been put to the test and been found wanting. *Pull yourself together*, was all she could think. *Stop beating yourself up.* That's what Clayton would have said.

CHAPTER TWENTY-SEVEN

Julie was engrossed in reading party-guest interviews on the system when her office phone rang. She didn't recognise the number but at this point in the Iverson investigation, she'd take any tip that came in.

The caller identified herself as Dr Jennifer Cooper, the pathologist whom she'd contacted about the cot death of Marianne Andrews.

"I hope I'm not disturbing you," she said. "But your phone call has had me thinking about the Marianne Andrews case. You did say that someone had mentioned to you possible parental abuse in connection with that case?"

"Yes I did."

"And could you tell me who that person was?"

"I'm afraid I didn't take down his name. It was a man I saw by the girl's grave in Happisburgh. It sounded like a rumour, and I wasn't talking to him in the context of work, so I didn't mention that I'm a police officer."

"I see. It's just that this is the first I've heard about possible parental abuse of the child, and I can't see anything in the records. The family wasn't on the radar of social services. But it's possible that families can slip through the gap, particularly in rural communities."

"I'm sorry, are you suggesting that we should investigate it now? Three months after she died?" Julie felt the nervousness bubble up in her throat. She was already imagining the impact on the parents. Would they have to dig up their child's grave? It was unthinkable.

"I'm just thinking that you could put some more skin on the bones, as it were. Thinking about this again, there was some bruising on the child's arms but this was explained as the father picking her up from the bed. He was distraught, obviously, and squeezed her. But maybe talk to the person you saw? Then the coroner could take a view about reopening the case."

Julie's head was filled with conflicting emotions. "I must say there was something I saw on social media that dated from the time of her death. But as there hadn't been a formal complaint it seemed pointless to continue. And there's another thing," she added. "My SIO doesn't like her officers going off the reservation. She made that clear to me on another case. I should probably have contacted you via our chief forensics officer."

"Fiona Blackhurst? Don't worry about her. I can set her straight," said Dr Cooper.

Julie hesitated before replying. If it hadn't been a cot death, she wouldn't have had the same interest in this case. But didn't she have enough on her plate at the moment?

Then she heard herself saying, "OK, fine. If you could bring Dr Blackhurst up to speed and get it cleared with my DCI, Charlotte Bligh, then I'll see what I can do."

* * *

Julie parked the Clio in her drive and took out two Sainsbury's bags from the back seat. She got to the front door before returning to the car to double-check that she'd locked it. Then performed the same ritual again. She drew a breath and unlocked the front door. She'd expected Ollie to be upstairs in his lair as usual, but he was in the sitting room. He seemed to be waiting for her.

"Hello, Chuckie. Is everything all right? School OK?" she asked.

"Yes," he said, flicking a curl from his forehead.

"Have you got one of your friends coming round?"

"No. Simon's coming tomorrow," he said.

"What about your homework?"

"I'm doing that after dinner."

"Well, help me unpack this, then," she said, taking the shopping bags into the kitchen.

He got up and followed her into the kitchen, where she noticed a pan on the hob containing freshly peeled potatoes.

"I didn't know what we were having for dinner but I thought we'd have potatoes," he said, by way of explanation. She smiled her appreciation. Things were looking up.

"Mum?" he said, taking out a bag of rice and reaching into an overhead cupboard to store it. She wondered, with slight dread, what might be coming.

"Yes, Ollie?"

"Meredith is pregnant with my sister." Ollie had his back to her so she couldn't see his face.

Julie knew that he was referring to Paul's girlfriend but her first thought was that Ollie already had a sister, his dead half-sister, Caroline. The idea of another baby girl unsettled her, although she'd never admit it. It somehow seemed like a rebuke, Meredith succeeding where she'd failed. And this announcement came only a month before Caroline's birthday on 29 October, which always triggered another round of heartache that she kept to herself for fear of upsetting Ollie. When the new sister came, she suspected that he'd forget all about Caroline, the sister that he'd never met but who lived on in her heart.

"That's nice," she said. "Do you want some juice?" She opened the fridge door and took out a pack of apple juice.

Ollie turned round, slightly flushed. "Is she my new mum?" he blurted out. Despite having abandoned calling her 'Mummy' in the last few months, presumably because he found it childish, Julie was touched by his vulnerability.

"Come here, you darling boy," she said. She put down the juice on the counter and gave him a big hug. "I'm your mummy, and I'm still here. And I always will be here for you." She held him by the shoulders so she could look into his dark eyes.

"You should count yourself lucky," she went on. "You've got me, your daddy and Meredith and soon a sister. You've got two families, like lots of other people, and we love you."

She hoped that this would be enough to reassure him. He'd suffered enough from the perceived rejection when Paul had deserted her for Meredith in the first place. Julie realised there would be twelve years between Ollie and his future sibling.

"Are you OK?"

"I suppose so." He twisted away from her. She wondered if he might be jealous.

"When's the baby due?" Julie asked. It was funny that Paul hadn't mentioned it. Fancy letting Ollie be the person to tell her. Maybe Paul thought it was none of her business. On the other hand, it must be him who'd described the baby as Ollie's 'sister'. She couldn't fault him for that.

"In the spring. I don't know when, exactly. I think they only just found out," he said.

"Well, that's lovely for them. And for you too." She squeezed his shoulder again. "Come on, let's finish unpacking." She held up an ice-cream carton retrieved from a shopping bag. "Look what we've got. Your favourite. Chocolate chip cookie dough."

He grinned. "Call me when dinner's ready?" He headed upstairs.

She put the ice cream in the freezer and went to the sink. She wiped away a tear from her cheek before beginning her handwashing ritual, which, she was convinced, would keep Ollie safe and give her a few moments of blessed relief.

CHAPTER TWENTY-EIGHT

Julie wandered over to the office window where rain was lashing down.

She peered down onto the car park and watched the ballet of cars, some arriving at the nick and others departing to a crime scene. She recognised Bullard's Renault nosing into a tight parking space and saw him squeeze out of the car. He gathered his jacket collar round his neck before running towards the entrance.

She was waiting at her desk when he appeared, shaking the raindrops from his hair like a dog.

"Seasonal weather at last," she commented. "Don't you have a brolly?"

"Brollies are for wimps," he said with a smile, then admitted, "I left it at home, actually — hadn't expected a downpour like this."

"How did you get on with Iverson senior?"

He sat down beside her and flicked through his notebook. "Oh, he just waved all the stuff about the villagers away. He said the Blackberry Lane residents are paranoid and uninformed. He explained that in recent years there have been a couple of major storm surges in Tideburgh which bit huge chunks out of the cliff face and caused the collapse. So he said the engineer who inspected the homes on the clifftop had no option but to act. He reckons that Iris Haggett's bungalow will be under threat when there's another big storm."

"Did you ask him about him being in talks with the owners of that house on Blackberry Lane about another plot?"

"Oh, yes." Bullard turned more pages and pointed at a line with his pen. "He said it's only a preliminary contact though. He'll have to find a developer, and also a farmer with land he's allowed to sell for construction. And he also mentioned that he's going to be retiring from the company anyway."

"Fair enough. So once again his neighbours have got the wrong end of the stick, have they?"

"And remember that if it did come to a planning application, he'd have to stand down and declare an interest when it was discussed by the council," said Bullard. He seemed to remember something else. "Oh, and he also mentioned that they've got a routine public meeting coming up in the next few days. I think it might be interesting for one of us to go along. We might pick up something."

"Very good. Although it might be more of the same," said Julie. "I mean, Mandy reported back that Iverson's fellow councillors corroborate his version about what happened before with his planning application." She was starting to feel a gnawing anxiety about how they could justify going down a rabbit hole that probably had nothing to do with Rupert Iverson's murder. Her email pinged. "The boss wants to see me," she said, pulling a face. "I'll catch up with you later."

* * *

Bligh was cleaning her specs when Julie arrived in her office. She held them up to the light after ensuring that all was to her satisfaction. She gestured to Julie to sit down.

"I hear from Fiona that you've been making enquiries into a completely unrelated case," she began.

Julie caught her brusque tone. "Well, that is, I didn't do it on purpose, ma'am," she said. And then, before she could stop herself, she was talking about Caroline's death and how her attention had been caught by the little girl's grave in Tideburgh.

Bligh's features softened as she listened. "I see. Given the nature of your own child's death, can you handle the Marianne Andrews case? I must stress that I only want you to look into the background for now. We're not talking about exhuming a dead child at this point."

"Yes, ma'am," said Julie. "Don't worry, I'll be fine."

"You're sure? I'm sorry for your loss. It must take a long time to heal, a sudden death like that."

"Quite sure." Julie was determined to show no emotion. "You never know, there may have been something we've overlooked in Tideburgh on the Iverson case anyway. I find it's often useful to return to the scene of a crime."

"Like criminals do," Bligh commented with a smile. "I'm still counting on forensics to find a match with the unidentified DNA samples on the broom and the bat. Dr Blackhurst tells me that Rupert Iverson's skull injury is consistent with a blow from a cricket bat, not a broom handle. So we need to figure out how the broom fits into the narrative."

* * *

Julie and Bullard settled down in their usual spot in a corner of the cafeteria with their coffees. The ficus beside them was as sad as ever. Bullard scoffed a Danish pastry while Julie was stirring her latte.

"I thought I'd better tell you," she said, "I've been asked to look into the possible suspicious death of a child in Tideburgh."

"Really?" said Bullard.

"It's not a secret, but it's a bit personal for me, you see," she said, explaining what she'd heard at the graveside of Marianne Andrews.

Bullard looked pained when she told him about Caroline. "That's terrible, losing a child. I can only imagine."

"You have daughters, don't you?" she asked.

"Yes. Two. One's five and the other is seven."

"Ah, that's sweet."

"You've not seen those two," he said. "What a handful!"

"And does your wife work?"

"Only part-time now. That way she can spend more time taking care of the kids. She's in sales so she can also work from home when necessary. But tell me, how are you going to go about finding out more about what happened to the girl?"

"I need to talk to the parents, obviously. And if possible, find the guy I saw outside the church who tipped me off about the rumours going round. I should track down the people who started these horrible rumours."

"Rumours travel fast round there, eh?" Bullard was frowning. He picked up his cup and swirled the liquid around before taking a long sip. "Sounds like you've got your work cut out for you. Let me know if you need any help."

"Thanks, Dave," she said, appreciative of the offer. "I was thinking of going over to the coast this afternoon, if the weather clears up. I can't help thinking that we're missing something about the Iverson murder."

"Talking of the Iversons, it seems that Rupert was quite popular in the village. The green activist I spoke to, Keith Hawkins, said he had some very good ideas about environmentally friendly buildings. Did you know he'd studied architecture at university?"

"Yes. But he dropped out before qualifying," said Julie.

"Well, apparently he'd kept up an interest, according to my guy. Rupert was saying that with Tideburgh being such a victim of climate change, the building industry needs to buck up."

"His dad's industry," said Julie. "I wonder if there were tensions there between father and son. But what do you think about where the investigation is going? We seem to be going round in circles at this point."

"I think our best chance is with forensics," he replied. "Unless we can work another angle, or if something new comes from the remaining interviews. But frankly, I think someone would have come forward by now, particularly given the press coverage."

Julie nodded slowly. "Maybe you're right," she said. She agreed with his analysis. Perhaps her judgement of him had been a little harsh. She realised it was his sense of entitlement that bothered her the most. What would Sam Clayton do now? she wondered.

CHAPTER TWENTY-NINE

Clayton answered the phone on the first ring.

"What's new, Julie?" he asked.

"How are you doing, yourself?" she replied.

"Up to my eyeballs in paperwork," he said. "I reckon I'll be back soon. I'll let the boss know. . . but what's happening on the Iverson case?"

"We're stuck," she said. "Honestly, we're running out of lines of enquiry and hoping that we can get a breakthrough with forensics." She explained about Rupert's fingerprints having been found on the broom at Richard Fairbairn's place. Not only had he already heard about that, but he'd also been briefed, presumably by Bligh, about the teenagers mixed up in Iris Haggett's death. He was aware that they'd been charged with manslaughter.

"OK. So what about if it was an intruder who got into Iverson Hall?" said Clayton. "Remember the padlocked gate in the back?"

"What do you mean?"

"I'm just thinking aloud, here, but isn't there a little caravan site in the village? Who stays there these days? There might be oddballs and drifters and people up to no good."

"People? You mean foreigners?" She'd picked up on his xenophobic undertone. "It's probably a local farmer who puts up fruit pickers during the season. But why would any of them kill Rupert Iverson on his birthday? Are you saying it was a motiveless crime?"

"I'm just saying, Julie. Your guess is as good as mine."

"Well, I suppose we shouldn't overlook that possibility," she said. "I'm going over there now, so I can check it out."

"Is Bullard behaving?" Clayton asked.

"Yes, he is, actually." Julie bristled. He was right, though; she could ask Bullard to check out the fruit pickers, after all. Why did she have to do everything?

"Is that it, boss?" she asked. Sometimes Clayton could be so annoying.

"Did you ever find out about the surprise that Bethany mentioned?"

"Surprise?"

"Yes, don't you remember, she said that Rupert had told her before the party that he had a surprise for her. Did nobody else mention that? Did Dennis Iverson know about it?"

Julie couldn't help thinking that she'd dropped the ball. This could be something significant, and they'd not followed up for days. What was Rupert's secret? Maybe he'd taken it to the grave.

"I'm on it, guv," she said. "See you soon."

* * *

By the time Julie reached Tideburgh the rainclouds had gathered and gloom had descended on the village.

She parked, as usual, in the car park overlooking the sea. White horses were being tossed by strong winds. The metal grey waves of the North Sea cascaded onto the beach. Julie walked round the car twice, double-checking that she'd left on the handbrake and that all the doors were locked.

Just as she was thinking that it was the first time she'd been to the village in bad weather, the heavens opened. Her umbrella was useless in the wind. She was halfway down Blackberry Lane and was already drenched. Where could she shelter? With her mac billowing around her, she sprinted back to the car and sat there until the squall had passed. Then she drove to the Smugglers Arms.

The pub was near deserted. The landlord was behind the bar, arranging pint glasses on a shelf behind him. He turned round as the door closed.

"It's been raining, I see," he said. She tried to pat her hair into place but instead it stuck together in rat's tails.

Raindrops dripped from her mac onto the stone floor.

"You're the police detective, aren't you? How are you getting on?" he added.

"We've not made any arrests yet, Mr Keeble, if that's what you mean."

"No. We've noticed that," he said. "Tough case to crack, is it? Murder at the manor? Sounds like there was a bit of an orgy over there." He laughed to himself and picked up a tea towel. Julie wondered whether his imagination had gone into overdrive about sex and wigs.

"You'll have seen, though, that three children from the village are suspected of involvement in Iris Haggett's death," Julie pointed out.

"Oh, yes. The whole village is talking about that," he replied. "What can I get you?"

Julie hesitated. "Actually, I was hoping that you might be able to help me contact somebody I met by the church in Happisburgh the other day. He was doing some work on the church exterior . . . it's a long shot, but . . ."

"There's only one person that could be," said the landlord. "Ron Archer. He does all the odd jobs, and he's a mason by trade so it's probably him."

"Does he live in Tideburgh, then?"

"Just outside, on the way to Happisburgh." He looked around for a piece of paper and wrote down an address.

"Here you go. He might be at home at this time. If it were a bit later, you'd find him in here."

Julie smiled and thanked him.

"Anything else I can do for you?" he asked. She wasn't sure if he was being sarcastic.

* * *

When she stepped outside the pub, the skies were blue and the air was filled with the fragrance of freshly watered grass. She couldn't figure out whether Simon Keeble was simply mocking the police efforts or whether his attitude was more hostile. What was certain was that village life must have been turned upside down by the two deaths, and maybe the locals had their own suspicions about who had killed Rupert Iverson. But if they did, they were keeping them to themselves.

She went back to the car and put Ron Archer's address into the GPS. It led her to a modern flintstone bungalow set back from the road behind a wall.

Just as she pulled over, the front door opened, and she recognised the man from the church graveyard.

"Mr Archer?" she called out. He didn't recognise her initially until she explained why she was back in Tideburgh.

"So you're a police officer?" he said, studying her warrant card. "I don't want to get anyone into trouble. There's enough of that round here at the moment."

"I'm just wondering whether you could tell me a bit more about Marianne Andrews. The little girl we were talking about in the churchyard. You mentioned that the neighbours were concerned after she died. The death notice says the parents live on Vicarage Road."

"They're not there anymore," he said. "That's what I heard anyway. She left him."

His words were jarring. It was like revisiting her own relationship after Caroline died.

"Oh. Have you any idea where I might find them now?"

"The father's still there. He's a farmer."

"On Vicarage Road?"

"That's right." Julie wondered whether he lived near Cathy and Rupert's smallholding. "Is there anything else?" she asked.

He shook his head. "Like I said . . ." he began.

"OK, well thanks anyway," she said, curtly. She hadn't expected more.

* * *

Julie drove back through Tideburgh. She was about to pass the smallholding but on impulse pulled into the drive. Maybe Cathy could help?

She found her in the vegetable patch, digging up potatoes. She watched her from a distance, forking the soil from the vegetables before lifting them into her wheelbarrow. Then she called out to her with a wave. Cathy waved back and left what she was doing, still carrying her fork.

"How's it going?" she asked. "Has there been a breakthrough in the case?"

"Not yet, I'm afraid. We're hoping that forensics can help out at this point."

Cathy seemed disappointed.

"Actually, I'm here on another matter. How well do you know Martin Andrews, your neighbour?"

"He's the one I told you about. The one who doesn't want to sell his land. He's a foul-mouthed bully, if you ask me," Cathy retorted.

"You are aware of what happened to his daughter?" Julie asked.

"Who isn't?" Cathy planted the fork into the soil. "Everyone round here thinks he did it."

Julie's eyes widened with astonishment. "You mean people think he killed her? Why would he do a thing like that?"

"A guy like that, I wouldn't put anything past him," she replied with a shrug. "They'd been separated for a while before Marianne died. Then he came back. And then the little girl died. Do you think that's a coincidence?"

Julie said nothing. Cathy continued, "Christine left soon after that. She took their other daughter with her straight after the funeral. She obviously couldn't stand being with him anymore."

"Have you any idea where Christine Andrews went to?"

"She went to stay with her parents in North Walsham. But I don't know where she is now. She didn't really keep in touch."

Julie sighed. She knew she had no option but to visit the farmer next door. She turned to go.

"Oh, by the way, there's just one more thing I wanted to check with you. Did you know if Rupert had any big plans for after the party? A big change in his life, maybe?"

Cathy seemed surprised by the question. "Nothing that he shared with me," she said, bitterly. "Maybe he was planning his new life with Bethany. Why would he tell me about that?"

CHAPTER THIRTY

Julie guided the Clio down a muddy track, dented by potholes, that led to a sprawling farmhouse through neatly harvested fields.

She heard a dog barking as soon as she stepped out of the car. A collie rushed out of a barn and began circling her as though rounding her up. Feeling slightly unnerved, she walked towards the barn where two young farmhands were filling crates from a pile of apples.

"Mr Andrews?" she asked.

One of them pointed towards the road and said, "He is coming. Potatoes."

She went back to the car to wait, followed by the dog, which soon lost interest when she stood motionless, leaning against the bonnet and scrolling on her phone. After about fifteen minutes, a tractor trundled into the yard, pulling a trailer loaded with potatoes.

A stocky man in his late forties climbed down from the tractor.

"You lost?" he said to Julie.

She took out her warrant card, asked if he was Martin Andrews, and explained that she wanted to talk to him about the death of his daughter.

"What about it?" He showed no emotion. He seemed to have something else on his mind. "I've only got a few minutes," he said. "The harvest this year has been a disaster. I think we can save the potato crop, but last year's flooding means that a lot of them were left in the ground. And the pea harvest was hit by the heatwave last month. This damned climate change is going to leave us farmers bankrupt!"

"Mr Andrews, I'd like you to just explain to me about what exactly happened when Marianne died. Was it you or your wife who found your daughter?"

He stared at her as though weighing up what to say. He rubbed some dirt from his windburned forehead before replying. "It was me. I got up at five as usual and I went into her room and found her."

"What made you realise she was dead? Did you touch her?"

"Yes, she was cold. Her face wasn't a normal colour. I shouted out to Christine and she came running and we dialled 999. That was about it."

"Do you remember if she was on her back or on her side?"

"Sorry, I can't remember. Maybe on her tummy. I just remember noticing she was stone cold when I put my hand on her face. I wasn't going to wake her, just stroke her, you know? I was on my way down to get my breakfast."

"I see. And had she shown any signs of discomfort previously?" Julie felt she was venturing into territory more suited to a social worker or medic than a detective.

"Not so far as I'm concerned, no. You'd have to ask Christine about that."

"I understand that you and Christine had been separated for a while?"

"Where did you hear that?" Andrews said, angrily. *It's all over social media.* Julie didn't respond.

"How can I leave my farm? It's my livelihood," he continued. "But if you must know, we did have a kind of trial separation that lasted a couple of weeks. I stayed with a mate in Tideburgh, but obviously carried on working on the farm. I can't just up sticks and go somewhere else! I came home because I wanted to patch things up with Christine."

"But I understand that she's no longer living here, correct?"

"Right." The farmer scratched his head and brushed some dust from his jeans. "And now, I've got to get on, OK?" He didn't look like the type to seek marital counselling, she thought.

"Of course. If you could just let me have an address for Christine?"

He shrugged. "I haven't the faintest idea. For some reason she blames me for the whole thing." He seemed to be struggling to keep control.

"Why would that be?"

"How should I know?" His voice was becoming more belligerent. Julie could easily imagine being battered by the muscles under his loose weave jumper.

"And your other daughter is with her? What's her name?"

"Alice."

"How old is she?"

"She's nine now," came the reply. He turned back to the tractor and grabbed the handhold. Julie realised her time was running out.

"I understand that some locals have taken to social media about what happened."

"You're a policewoman, aren't you?" he bellowed. "You should find out who's behind that whispering campaign and lock them up! I'm just trying to run my farm in a fight to the death with the weather, without any help from anyone. Goodbye, Detective."

"Mr Andrews, would you mind giving me your phone number in case I have to get in touch with you again?"

He spat out a string of numbers that she managed to take down before he climbed inside his tractor cab. He gave her a wave as he took his potato load through the farmyard.

She got back into her mud-spattered car and headed to the nick. She wanted to check whether Kevin Fuller was still in the office. Perhaps he could help her identify the person behind the @justiceformarianne Twitter account that had circulated the rumours about the death of Marianne.

What if we misjudged Cathy? she thought as she sped along the Norwich outer ring. She'd certainly seen another side to the wronged girlfriend today. What if Cathy had plotted revenge against Rupert for being unfaithful? She'd been at the manor with a perfect opportunity, and everyone in fancy dress, after all. But who could she have had as an accomplice?

Julie sighed. She felt pummelled by the hostility that the villagers had shown her that day, particularly Andrews, who seemed like a brute. But just because he was a brute didn't mean he was a child killer, did it?

CHAPTER THIRTY-ONE

The next morning, Julie was among the first in the detective suite to be seated at her workstation.

Bullard strolled in about half an hour later and went straight to her desk.

"How did you get on in Tideburgh?" he asked.

Julie pulled a face. "So-so," she said. "I need to track down Marianne's mother and then frankly someone else can decide whether they want to dig up a dead child. But it turns out the girl's father lives next door to Cathy Swinson, Rupert's partner. He's the farmer who refused to sell them some land next to their market garden. And Cathy seems to think he's a piece of shit."

He sat down and pushed up his sleeves. Julie hadn't noticed before that he had tattoos on both forearms.

"Interesting. And do you agree?" he asked.

"I have no opinion," she said with a smile. "I'd keep my distance, though, from Martin Andrews. He's a big strong guy full of resentment. But then if he's been accused of something he didn't do then he'd be right to feel resentful, wouldn't he? And he's obviously stressed out because of the weather as well."

"The weather?"

"Yes. He was going on about climate change and how it's no good for farming."

"Tell me about it," he said. "My family were farmers. Dad was the foreman on a farm outside Lowestoft and he did nothing but complain about the weather."

"Well, I wish you'd have been there yesterday," said Julie. "But could you go back to Tideburgh today? There's another angle on the Iverson case that might be worth exploring."

Bullard shot her a look that seemed to say, *Is there no end to this investigation?* He said, "What's the angle?"

"An intruder. There's an outside chance that it might have been one of the pickers who are staying at the caravan site. Can you go over there?"

"Yes, boss," he said.

"By the way, Dave, did you ever ask Dennis Iverson about the surprise that Bethany Price mentioned to us? She said that Rupert had a surprise for her and was to tell all after the party. But then he never did, of course. I asked Cathy about it yesterday and she wasn't very helpful."

"I don't think I was there for that interview," he said.

Julie frowned. Wasn't he keeping up on the system? "OK, I need to go round to see him anyway," she said. "And by the way, did we get a DNA sample from Cathy?"

"I'll check."

Julie watched Bullard walk over to his desk. She was prepared to bet that he'd head down to the canteen to get a coffee before starting his day. Sure enough, he hung his jacket on the back of his chair and kept on going towards the door. She felt resentful, put upon and a tiny bit jealous. And he hadn't even bothered to ask her if she wanted one.

She was about to pick up the phone on her desk when it rang. It was Kevin Fuller.

"Can you come down?"

"On my way," she replied.

She found Kevin in his office surrounded by mysterious pieces of equipment which he used to unlock the secrets of the criminal world.

He swivelled round to face her, his eyes enlarged by his thick-lensed glasses. "That was easy, for a change."

"So who does that Twitter account belong to?" she asked.

"Somebody called Cathy Swinson," he said.

"Cathy!" she exclaimed. "Doesn't she realise how easy it is to trace an account? What if she's been making completely unsubstantiated accusations?"

"Do you want the identities of the accounts who were retweeting what she wrote?" Kevin asked.

"Why not?" said Julie. "Let's expose that whole toxic network in the village."

She walked slowly along the corridor and back up the stairs to her desk. Could it be that Rupert Iverson's murder and the death of Marianne Andrews were about to become inextricably linked?

* * *

Dennis Iverson was parking the Tesla outside his house when Julie's car nosed through the gate.

"Come in, come in, detective," he said, ushering her inside. He hung his keys on a set of hooks in the hall. "The wind's bitter today."

Suzanna was sitting by the French windows and waved when they entered the living room.

"So how can we help you today?" Dennis asked, as Suzanna sent Dange to bring tea and biscuits.

"I'm wondering whether you know anything about Rupert telling Bethany that he'd give her a surprise after the birthday party," said Julie.

Both the Iversons looked puzzled. "A surprise? What sort of surprise?" Suzanna asked. At the very same moment, Dennis said, "Bethany? Why would he have a surprise for Bethany?"

Julie hesitated before plunging in. "Well, Mr Iverson, were you aware that Rupert and Bethany had got back together again?"

"Oh, really?" he said. "That's wonderful. I had no idea — did you, darling?"

Suzanna shook her head. "Absolutely not. We liked her, didn't we?"

"Oh, yes," said Dennis. "They were always a good match, those two. Do you know how long they'd been back together? He and Cathy were living together . . ."

"A few months, apparently," said Julie. "Cathy had found out, so it was all a bit awkward. It seems that Bethany finished with her boyfriend on the night of Rupert's party."

"So could the surprise have been a proposal of marriage from Rupert?" Dennis asked.

"Honestly, we don't know. It could be that he took his secret to the grave with him. But can we go back to the last time you saw him, Mr Iverson? Not the night of the party — I know you didn't have the chance to talk then — I mean the day before."

"Of course. It was the night before the party, wasn't it, dear?" He checked the detail with his wife, who nodded.

"What did you talk about on that evening? It might be important."

Dange appeared carrying a tray of cups of tea and a plate of biscuits, which she arranged on the heavy coffee table. Dennis thanked her and waited until she was out of earshot before saying, "It's funny, isn't it, that he never mentioned Bethany to us?"

"Maybe he thought we'd be upset because of Cathy," said Suzanna, picking up her cup and staring into it.

"Mr Iverson? So do you remember your conversation that night?"

"Yes, we talked about his interest in environmentally conscious houses, smart houses, that sort of thing. And in the course of the evening I invited him to take over as head of my company."

"Head of the company? What was his response?" Julie asked.

"Well, he said he wanted to think about it. He was going to give me his answer the day after the party," said Dennis, shaking his head.

"Mr Iverson, why didn't you mention this to us before?" Julie demanded.

He looked surprised. "But why should I? It was family business. You don't think it sheds any light on his murder, do you? On the contrary, it meant he was in good spirits for his fancy-dress party, and I suspect that he was going to accept. At least I hoped he would. But that's why I didn't share it with anyone, not even Jeremy."

Julie put down her pen and asked, "Is it possible that this was the surprise he was going to reveal to Bethany?"

The Iversons looked at each other. "I suppose it's possible, yes," said Dennis.

Julie looked down at her notes, her brain spinning.

Suzanna Iverson cleared her throat. "Why don't you tell DS Everett, dear . . . ?"

Dennis took a sip of tea from his porcelain cup before setting it down on the saucer.

"The reason I spoke to Rupert was because I'm ill. Dying, in fact," he said.

Julie was so shocked that for a moment she didn't know what to say, and she gasped. "Oh. I'm so sorry," she said.

He raised a hand in acknowledgement. "The fact is that I've been diagnosed with cancer, and it's terminal, I'm afraid. My doctor doesn't know how long I have but he basically told me to put my affairs in order. That's why I spoke to Rupert."

"I see," said Julie. "Mr Iverson, I'm so terribly sorry to hear about all this."

"So now do you understand why I didn't mention it before? It's just not relevant to the investigation."

I'll be the judge of that, thought Julie.

"Very well," she said. "If you think of anything else, no matter what, that might help us find Rupert's killer, I'd be grateful."

"But why haven't you arrested anybody?" Suzanna seemed quite agitated. "We read that it might have been a homophobic attack. And we were told by your superior that you have the murder weapon!" She leaned back in her wheelchair and passed a hand across her forehead, fixing Julie with an ice-blue stare.

"But darling," Dennis said, "Rupert wasn't gay. And what we've just heard about Bethany proves it, doesn't it?"

"Yes, but it would still be a homophobic attack if his attacker *thought* he was gay. I mean, it was a fancy-dress party after all. We all saw that photograph in the newspaper," she said with a sigh.

Julie leaned forward. "Mrs Iverson, we have absolutely no evidence that Rupert was killed in a homophobic attack. I'm sorry that you've been hurt by these unfounded rumours. And yes, we do have the murder weapon. We're quite confident that we will be able to identify Rupert's killer from trace DNA found on it. You can be reassured that we're moving forward on the investigation." Julie wished she felt as confident as she sounded. But her remarks seemed to calm Suzanna.

"I understand. But this is a living nightmare for us," she replied. "A living nightmare."

CHAPTER THIRTY-TWO

Clayton walked through the detective suite as though he didn't have a care in the world.

"Morning," he said to Julie, placing a pink stick of Blackpool rock on her desk. She looked up in surprise.

"What did you expect? Mushy peas?" he said.

"Thanks, Sam, I'll give it to Ollie," she replied. "Welcome back."

"I've got a couple more for Bullard's kids, just so no one's jealous." He dropped onto the seat next to her. His few days off had obviously done him some good, she thought.

"How was the funeral?" she asked.

He pulled a face. "Grim. It pissed with rain and there was only me and an uncle there, and two or three of Dad's friends with their walking frames. I suppose that's what happens when you get to his age. And he was a bad-tempered old fart so he didn't have many friends anyway."

Julie laughed.

"I've got his ashes in the car boot, actually," he went on. She was surprised he was confiding such personal information.

"Did he leave instructions?"

"No, that's the problem. There's a quiet place where we scattered my mum's ashes on the coast near Lancaster, but the local council has ruined it since then by trying to turn it into a tourist attraction. I'll probably go up to the Lakes with him instead. Anyway, how goes it here?"

She told him about her conversation with the Iversons.

"Wow," he said. "Poor guy. Stands to reason he wouldn't tell anyone, I suppose. What if Rupert had turned him down? I guess Jeremy would have been next in line. Remember he told us he's the 'son' in 'Iverson and Son'?"

"Yes, you're right," she said. "But in the meantime, I can't get it out of my mind that Cathy might have killed Rupert out of jealousy."

"Well, she's a strapping country lass. But what makes you say that? She's likely going to have to leave that small-holding now that Rupert's gone."

"She'd have had to leave it anyway, if she broke up with him." Julie filled him in on the Marianne Andrews case and Cathy's tweets to the father of the dead girl.

"I'm sorry I didn't mention this before, but it's a bit personal, as you can imagine," she said. "I'm doing a report for Bligh on whether to open a case on Marianne Andrews."

"Sure."

"Anyway, the father is the same farmer who refused to sell land to Cathy and Rupert so they could expand their business. I must say it made me look at her in a different way. She's no goody two-shoes," said Julie. "I want to see the mother, though, to see what she has to say. She's in North Walsham."

"And what's Bullard been up to?"

Julie sensed a presence and looked round. "Talk of the devil," she said.

Bullard accepted his sticks of rock from Clayton with a big smile. "Back in the saddle?" he asked. "Everything OK?"

"Yes, absolutely," said Clayton. "All done and dusted. What's your latest?"

Bullard pulled a face. "I interviewed a bunch of fruit pickers yesterday afternoon. First of all, hardly any of them speak English. None of them had heard of Iverson Hall, they don't have cars, and the caravan site is all the way on the other side of the village. So frankly it's beyond me how any of them would have had the idea of driving there in the middle of the night to kill Rupert Iverson, who they'd never even heard of. And what was the motive? Robbery? I suppose it could have been a burglary gone wrong, but nothing was stolen from the house, was it?"

He looked meaningfully at Julie. She was sorry for wasting his time. Maybe she shouldn't have listened to Clayton in the first place.

"Well, we need to explore every avenue," she said, with a sideways glance at Clayton who had put on his 'who, me?' face. "Where are they from?"

"Poland, Bulgaria, Romania, you name it," he said. "The Poles had quite good English. But with the others it was painful."

She remembered the two farmhands working for Martin Andrews. If they were going down the route of questioning all the foreigners around the village in the hope of finding an unknown intruder, they should talk to them too. But what was the point? Bullard was right. It smacked of desperation.

"Right, well I'm going to let you two catch up. I've got to clear things up with Christine Andrews in North Walsham."

She noticed Bullard's quizzical look at Clayton.

"See you later." She picked up her bag.

"Oh, by the way," said Clayton. "I hear on the grapevine that Jonathan Murray has been done for assault against James Crofton."

So her theory had been correct that Jonathan must have found out about his relationship with Brian, and then taken revenge on the lover.

She wondered how Clayton had found out. As she walked to the lift, she realised he must have been talking to his mate at the *Eastern Daily Press*.

* * *

Julie found Christine Andrews at an address on King's Arms Street in North Walsham. Her house was a modest white-washed maisonette.

A small, overweight woman came to the door on the first knock. Julie showed her warrant card and said, "Mrs Andrews? it's about Marianne."

"What about her?" she said, on the defensive. "I've not got long, I'm on my break. I work at Lidl," she added, by way of explanation.

She led Julie into a small front room, which was right on the pavement. The room had net curtains to prevent passers-by from staring in. They sat in the two armchairs in front of an electric fire.

"Is your daughter here?" Julie enquired.

"No. She's at school. Why? Do you need to see her?"

"No. Not at this point. As you'll be aware, there's been a bit of a campaign in Tideburgh to get what they call 'justice for Marianne'. There are rumours going round that she might not have died accidentally. Can you tell me exactly what happened on the morning she died?"

Mrs Andrews sighed. She was in her early forties, younger than her estranged husband. But where he was toned from his outdoor physical work, she was pudgy with soft upper arms and swollen ankles above her slippers.

"It was Martin who found her when he went down to breakfast. He'd always look in on the kids when he went down."

"Did Marianne have her own room?"

"Yes. She'd been in her own bedroom for about a year. Alice had the bedroom across the corridor from her. Anyway he went in and the first I knew was that I was being woken up by him shouting. I'll never forget it. He was shaking her, telling her to wake up — it was awful." Mrs Andrews took a paper tissue tucked into her skirt and dabbed her eyes.

She sighed again. "I rushed in and picked her up from her cot and could feel her little body was completely cold. I ran down and called 999. And that was it."

"You're probably aware that sudden unexplained death in childhood is quite a rare occurrence in children aged more than a year old?" She wasn't going to mention her own experience.

"Yes. But that's what they said it was," Mrs Andrews replied.

"But you thought that it might not have been an accident? Why are people asking for justice for Marianne?"

"Because it was Martin who'd put her to bed on the night she died. I reckon he left her face down on the pillow when she went to sleep. And she was found lying on her tummy the next day — dead!"

"Did you go in to check on her before you went to bed?"

"I did. But I only peeked through the door and didn't go over to her cot. She always slept very well so I wasn't worried. And then the next thing I hear is him screaming that she's dead!"

"Was Mr Andrews ever rough with Marianne? Had she ever had bruising?"

She shook her head slowly. "No. I was the one he knocked around."

"Did you ever report him?"

"Report him? To the police?" The thought seemed never to have occurred to her. "He had a violent temper, that's all. He'd hit me if his dinner wasn't on the table the minute he got in from the fields, so I made sure that everything was just so in the house. I'm not an idiot. The day that Marianne died, he pushed me onto the bed so hard that I hit my head on the bedstead."

"And why did he do that?"

"Because he was shouting at me to shut up!"

"I heard that the two of you had separated for a while, before Marianne died. I heard that Mr Andrews left the house."

Mrs Andrews raised her eyebrows in surprise. "Well, yes. I summoned up the courage to tell him to get out. But I let him come home after a couple of weeks, maybe less. He was hanging around on the farm anyway, because of his work, trying to make up."

"Tell me, Mrs Andrews, is Cathy Swinson a friend of yours?"

"Yes, she was our neighbour. Terrible what happened to Rupert. I read about it in the paper."

"So are you aware that Cathy is behind the campaign to get justice for Marianne?"

Mrs Andrews glanced down at her watch. "I've only got a few minutes. I have to get back to work. But she was only trying to help me. She knew all about Martin's behaviour. I suppose I might have said something about how I blamed him for Marianne's death. Maybe she overreacted a bit . . . there was certainly no love lost between the two of them, anyway." Her voice trailed off.

"I see. And you were aware, were you, that Mr Andrews had refused to sell some of your land to Rupert and Cathy?"

"Yes, of course."

Julie put away her notebook. "So could you please tell me why you moved out?"

"I just felt that with him behaving like a bear with a sore head, Alice and I weren't safe in the house with him anymore. I'd sit looking at him across the table, and sometimes I wanted to die, to be with Marianne. He never spoke about her ever again after the funeral. I suppose that's how he coped with it. But I couldn't handle it."

She dabbed her eyes again with the crumpled tissue. Julie reached across to touch her hand.

"Did you get any counselling after Marianne died?" she asked.

"Counselling? No. I don't see what difference that would have made. They can't bring her back, can they?"

"I'm so, so sorry, Mrs Andrews," Julie said. She noticed a photograph on the mantelpiece of a toddler in a dress sitting on a rug in a garden. "Is that her?"

"Yes. I took that picture outside the farm."

Mrs Andrews showed Julie out and she returned to her car, which was parked round the corner. She sat there gripping the car keys for a few minutes, deep in thought. Then she took out her phone in case there were any messages. There was one from Clayton asking her to check in.

"It's me, guv, what's up?" she asked.

"Can you come straight back? It's about Cathy. Her prints are on the broom handle and the cricket bat that was thrown into the sea."

CHAPTER THIRTY-THREE

Could Cathy be Rupert's murderer?

As Julie drove back to the nick, she remembered how Cathy's jealousy of Bethany had bubbled up in their last conversation. If jealousy was the motive, the opportunity to seek revenge could have arisen on the night of the party.

But surely Cathy couldn't have attacked Rupert without an accomplice. Who could have helped her? She remembered what Bligh had said about the drowning being tantamount to waterboarding. Could that have been the tactic to force Rupert to abandon his new relationship with Bethany? That didn't seem likely.

Julie remembered Cathy's grief only hours after the murder. Could she really be someone who could put on such an act after killing Rupert in cold blood? She simply didn't believe it. But if not Cathy, then who? They really were running out of options in this case.

Her thoughts turned back to Christine Andrews. So far as she could make out, Marianne's mother was casting around for a culprit based on her feelings of guilt. Julie remembered her own guilt after finding the body of her eighteen-month-old daughter, and how it had also driven her and her husband apart. Unlike Christine Andrews, she'd never actually accused him of responsibility, although if she were honest, each of them probably believed that the other was to blame.

She switched on the radio to take her mind off things. It was the top of the hour, and the Radio Norfolk news was reporting that Jonathan Murray had been arrested for assault in the case of the homophobic attack in Norwich. *Why are they still talking about a homophobic attack? It was nothing of the sort!* It had to be jealousy. She hit the off button.

It was only as she was driving through Wroxham that she was struck by the realisation that the reason she had developed her compulsive disorder was doubtless because of her deep-seated feeling that she'd failed to keep Caroline safe — all this time she'd put it down to work stress, suppressed guilt and lingering grief. The behavioural therapist whom she'd consulted a couple of years ago had told her that OCD could be partly genetic in origin. But she'd never led her to the explanation that it was her guilt over Caroline which meant that she was determined to keep Ollie safe, by whatever means possible.

Ten minutes later she was hanging up her jacket and scarf in the detective suite. She hadn't been able to stop herself returning to the car from reception to check that she'd locked it, and worried that one of her colleagues might be watching from an upstairs window, and maybe mocking her. *I have to get this under control*, she thought to herself. But she was powerless to do so.

Upstairs in the detective suite, she caught sight of Clayton at his workstation.

"All reet?" he greeted her.

"Yes. I'm going to recommend to Bligh that we don't take the Marianne Andrews case any further. What's this about Cathy?" she asked.

"She's on her way in. The boss got the call from Fifi about the trace DNA on the brush. There are quite a few other samples which remain unidentified on the cricket bat too."

"Trace DNA?" said Julie. "That could be tricky, couldn't it?" They both knew that such small amounts of

DNA samples retrieved from crime scenes were far from the gold standard and often threw up false positives.

Clayton shrugged. "Look, we'll see what Cathy says."

Julie glanced around the office. "Where's Dave?"

"I let him take a break as I've asked him to go to the district council meeting with the Tideburgh residents tonight. We're still turning over every stone, Julie."

* * *

Cathy was seated next to a duty solicitor in the interview room. She stiffened when Clayton thanked her for attending voluntarily. When he informed her that she was being interviewed under caution on suspicion of murder, she burst into tears.

"What are you talking about?" she sobbed. "Are you seriously suggesting that I killed Rupert?"

"Cathy, we need to hear your side of the story. This is an opportunity to fill in some of the gaps for us," said Julie.

"But I've told you my side of the story, as you call it. What else do you need to know?" Her voice was strangled with emotion.

"Your fingerprints have been found on a broom handle and on the cricket bat which was used in the attack," said Clayton. "What's your explanation for that?"

"What?" she repeated. "I can't believe I'm hearing this. Oh my God!"

She turned to the solicitor who said something to her in a low voice. Julie wondered whether she was reminding her of her right to remain silent. Whatever she'd said, her words seemed to have a soothing effect.

"If you mean why would I be using a broom, there was one in the summer house by the pool," Cathy said, wiping her eyes. "On the morning of the party, just before lunch, in fact, it was a nice day and Rupert and I had a swim. We'd got to the house early that morning. Before we went into the pool, I took the cushions outside to dry them on the sun loungers as it was a lovely clear day. And I swept the dirt off the paving stones around the pool, as we had bare feet."

"What did you do with the broom?" Julie asked.

"I put it back in the summer house."

Julie and Clayton looked at each other.

"Are you sure?"

"Yes. Why?"

"Because that's not where it was found."

She looked perplexed.

"Now, Cathy, what about the cricket bat?" Julie asked.

"Oh, that's quite simple," said Cathy. "In the afternoon, a few of us played cricket in the field outside the house."

"You were the umpire, I seem to recall," said Julie. "And umpires don't handle the bat."

"No, of course. But at the end of the game, when we went back inside, I picked up one of the bats and left it in the summer house. We put both the bats and the wickets in there."

"Cathy, thanks so much for coming in," said Julie. "That's really helpful."

"Is that it?" Cathy asked, before standing up. She seemed surprised that the interview had been so short.

"Yes." Clayton switched off the recorder. "Thanks for helping with our enquiries. Please let us know if there's anything else you remember that could help with the investigation."

The two detectives followed the two women to reception and watched them leave.

"Shall we grab a coffee?" Clayton asked her.

"Just give me a minute. I want to talk to Cathy about something. Mine's a latte, please," she said with a smile.

She went outside and waited at a discreet distance until the solicitor had said goodbye to Cathy. Julie sidled up to her as she reached her car.

"Do you have a sec, Cathy?"

"Why, is there something else you want to accuse me of?"

"I've been talking to the parents of Marianne Andrews about the death of their daughter. I believe you know what I'm talking about."

"Why, what's happened?" Cathy shot back.

"I just want to warn you that you can't go round circulating unsubstantiated accusations against people. I happen to know that you're behind the 'justice for Marianne' account on Twitter."

"You can't do that!" Cathy protested. "That's a private account."

"We got a court order," Julie lied. "And there are grounds to have your account shut down."

"What do you mean, unsubstantiated accusations?" Cathy was staring defiantly at Julie. "That's not what Chrissie Andrews says."

"I've spoken to her and there is nothing to indicate that she has accused her husband of killing their child. She says that you exaggerated what she said because of your grudge against Mr Andrews."

"Ha!" Cathy said. "So that's it."

She put her hand in her pocket to dig out her keys. "Have you finished?" she said.

"Yes. Have a nice day," said Julie, turning on her heel. She heard the car door slam behind her.

She walked back into the nick with a smile on her face. She'd write up her report that evening to Bligh, recommending that no further action should be taken to investigate a suspicious death in the case of Marianne Andrews.

She strolled into the canteen where Clayton was seated at their usual table in the corner.

"Does anyone ever water that poor plant?" She gestured in the direction of the desiccated ficus.

"Not my department," he said, grinning. "One latte, madam."

"Thanks." She sat down.

"What was all that about?"

"Oh, nothing much. I just told Cathy that actions have consequences if she wants to keep stirring up trouble over Marianne Andrews. I'm going to tell Bligh it's not worth pursuing."

"Oh? Good," he said. "Anyway she's probably off the hook, in the Iverson case, isn't she? Now we know the killer, or killers, picked up the broom and the bat in the summer house, then left the property by the back gate and chucked them both over the cliff."

"Mm," said Julie, nursing her coffee. "Isn't it funny, though, that none of them heard any noise from the pool? No voices, no struggle, not even a splash."

"Yes, but with the windows closed, plus the distance? Plus the fact that it was in the middle of the night and they were all pissed out of their minds—"

"Except Rupert," Julie interjected.

"Yes, except him. Anyway I suppose it's not that surprising."

Clayton took a last slurp of his coffee and put down the cup, eyeing the dry patches on Julie's hands.

"Yes, it's started again," she said, sheepishly. "But I'm dealing with it."

He acknowledged her words with a sympathetic nod of the head.

"I'll check with Fifi if they've got any interesting footprint analysis from that night which could back up our case. Although we'd have heard by now if they had, I reckon. And of course there's still the mystery trace DNA on the broom and the bat."

"This case," sighed Julie. "Every lead goes up in smoke."

CHAPTER THIRTY-FOUR

Julie settled behind her laptop on the kitchen table to draft her report to Bligh.

Ollie was upstairs doing his homework, after helping her with the washing-up. She'd listened in silence as he burbled on about the football match he'd attended with his father. She'd noticed that the clothes now left in tidy piles around his bedroom included a Norwich City T-shirt.

Now, all was quiet.

As she lifted the lid of her computer, her mobile rang. Julie sighed in annoyance. She didn't recognise the caller ID but picked up anyway.

"Detective Sergeant, this is Suzanna Iverson speaking. I'm so sorry to disturb you at home but I've been thinking about our conversation."

"That's fine, Mrs Iverson, don't worry about it. How can I help?" said Julie.

"I'm afraid I can't get something off my mind since your last visit. It may be nothing, in fact I hope it is, but it may be something terrible."

Julie was taut with attention. She let Suzanna continue.

"Do you remember that my husband said he didn't tell anyone about his offer to Rupert to take over the company?"

"Yes."

"Well, the thing is, I had supper with Jeremy at the house on the evening of the party. I wasn't able to go and Jeremy came over to keep me company, as you know. I'm afraid that during the course of the evening, I let the cat out of the bag."

"What exactly did you tell him?"

"About his father's illness. I felt we owed it to him to tell him the truth. And then it just slipped out about Rupert and the firm. I hadn't expected Jeremy would be so upset but he absolutely hit the roof. He was ranting and raving, said it was so unfair, Rupert got everything, et cetera. He was incandescent. I must say I was taken aback. The reason I'm calling you is . . . " She came to a halt and there was a long pause.

"Yes, Mrs Iverson?"

"Well, I never thought that my own son could do such a thing, but I've come to the belief that I couldn't rule it out, having seen his behaviour that night. What do you think?"

"From what you're saying, he could have had a motive to take Rupert's life so that he'd never take over the firm. But didn't you corroborate his story about him not leaving your house that night?"

"Yes, but just because we never heard him leave doesn't mean that he didn't go out, does it?"

"No, indeed. But could he get into Iverson Hall? I remember him telling us that he doesn't have a key."

"I don't know whether he does or not. But I was thinking about that, and it would be simple for him to pick up my husband's keys from a hook in the hall of our house, and then put them back on his return."

"I see. Is there anything else, Mrs Iverson? Are you prepared to make a formal statement about what you just told me?"

"Is that strictly necessary? I haven't mentioned this to my husband. He was very insistent on keeping the information about Rupert confidential. He'll be furious if I tell him. In fact he's out at a meeting in Tideburgh at the moment, which is why I was able to ring you without him knowing."

Julie began to wonder if Suzanna had thought through the consequences of her confession. "We really need you to do that, yes. And we're going to have to bring Jeremy in for questioning, of course."

"Very well. Yes, understood," she said.

Julie sensed that she wanted to say more. "Is there anything else, Mrs Iverson?"

"As a matter of fact, there is. Again, it might be nothing, but the next morning, I mean on the morning after the party, Jeremy left before breakfast. There's nothing strange in that, but I went into the living room with Dange just as he was putting on his jacket to leave, and I noticed that he wasn't wearing the same trousers as the night before."

"And why would that be unusual?"

"It's just that he didn't have an overnight bag with him — he keeps his toilet things at the house for his visits but not clothes. Anyway he was wearing a pair of jeans and it struck me that they were slightly too big for him."

"Had you seen these jeans before?"

"That's the point, I hadn't noticed him wearing them before. I'm only mentioning this in case you might think it's significant, that's all. I'd never forgive myself if Rupert's murder is never solved, even if the truth is unbearable." Her voice trembled with emotion. Suzanna Iverson had been grappling with a terrible dilemma.

After she had ended the call, Julie stared at her phone in disbelief before dropping it onto the table. This was a turn-up for the books. Jeremy Iverson had been hiding in plain sight from the beginning.

She picked up the phone again and rang Clayton, who answered straight away.

"Sorry to bother you, boss. But Suzanna Iverson just dobbed in her son for murdering his brother."

CHAPTER THIRTY-FIVE

Jeremy Iverson was brought to the nick before eight the next morning.

He'd requested the presence of his solicitor, Catherine McKinsey, who only appeared an hour later, after DNA samples had been taken.

Clayton and Julie were waiting for them in the interview room.

Clayton read out the caution to Jeremy, informing him that he was being questioned on suspicion of the murder of his brother. The suspect didn't bat an eyelid. *Game on.*

Clayton ran through the details of what Jeremy had previously told them.

"You said that you stayed at your parents' home on the night of the party, and that you went to bed after the ten o'clock news. Is there anything in your statement that you'd like to change?"

Jeremy cast his blue eyes up to the ceiling, as though considering his response.

"Mr Iverson, I'd remind you that your prior statement may be used in evidence against you. It's important that we have a truthful record. Do you understand?" said Clayton.

"Yes," came the reply.

"Did you leave the Norwich house at any point on the night of Rupert's party?"

Jeremy's gaze slid towards his solicitor before he replied, "No comment."

"And do you remember the subject of your conversation with your mother on that evening?"

He shook his head. "I can't say that I do. Sorry."

"Allow me to refresh your memory. She informed you that your father had decided to step back from the company and had invited Rupert to take charge."

"And what of it?" said Jeremy.

"We hear that you flew into a jealous rage on hearing this information."

"I was obviously upset, yes. As I mentioned to you, I'd been led to believe that I would be taking over the company from my father. That's why he'd renamed it Iverson and Son."

"Yes, but it seems he had a change of mind after hearing that he had terminal cancer."

Jeremy Iverson sighed. He looked at his solicitor again, before leaning forward and saying, "Excuse me, but if I've been woken up at six thirty to be brought to this police station to answer questions about whether I murdered my own brother, you'd better come up with something better than this."

He leaned back in his chair before adding, "Where's the proof? Are you seriously expecting to convict me because I flew into a rage on hearing that my brother was going to replace my father as head of the family company? And I would add that he hadn't actually accepted the offer when he died."

Julie fixed Jeremy with a stare and said, "I'm going to ask you one more time. Did you leave the house in Norwich at any point on the night of the party?"

"No comment," he said.

"OK," she said. "Maybe you could tell us a little more about your relationship with Rupert. You mentioned in your earlier statement that you weren't close."

"That's true. That's all I have to say on the matter."

There was a short silence before the solicitor intervened. "We seem to be going round in circles here. Is there any point in keeping my client here any longer?"

"Just one more thing, Mr Iverson," Julie interjected. "Do you play cricket?"

"No, why? My brother's the sportsman, as you probably are aware," he responded without hesitation.

"And is this a social question or relevant to the investigation?" McKinsey said.

"I was wondering whether Mr Iverson might have any information about the cricket match that took place outside the manor on the afternoon before his brother's death," Julie said.

"No more than I saw in the papers," he replied. "As you know, I wasn't invited to the party. So if you're talking about the missing cricket bat that I read about, I can't help you there." He glanced at his solicitor as though to say, "we're done here".

"Let's take a short break," said Clayton for the tape before he and Julie left the room.

"What do you want to do?" Julie asked.

"I'll have to ask the boss but I want to keep him here. I don't want him intimidating his mother at this point. He's a bloody cool customer, isn't he?"

"I guess we're back to waiting for forensics. But if it's his DNA on that cricket bat, that would bolster the case against him," she said. "He must feel pretty confident that the bat was never recovered from the sea."

"Yes. That was a good question you threw in there. How long will it take to get that DNA analysis? Damn!" Clayton exclaimed.

"We could ask to keep him in for twenty-four hours and use the time to find out as much as we can about him from his parents. I seem to remember there's a sister too, who wasn't at the party. And in the meantime maybe Fifi can make sure that Jeremy's DNA analysis is treated as a priority."

"You're right." Clayton took out his phone. "And wasn't he divorced? Why are we only doing this now?" Julie knew that he was kicking himself and that his remarks weren't meant to criticise her.

"I'll deal with this," he added. "But from now, every minute counts."

* * *

Julie went up to the detective suite where she found Bullard seated at his workstation.

"Hi. How did it go?" he asked.

Julie pulled a face. "Let's say that we've got our work cut out for us today, assuming that we can keep Jeremy Iverson here for a bit. What about you? How was the meeting last night?"

"Dennis Iverson was in the firing line," he said. "A couple of other council members were there as well but he was the one who came in for the criticism because he's the coastal management team chair. After a while it got quite personal. One of the villagers accused him of bringing shame to the village."

"What on earth for?"

"Oh, he talked about the 'despicable behaviour' of party guests at Iverson Hall, not to mention what happened when his son was murdered. One of them said, let me check—" he flicked through his notebook — "oh yes, one of them said, 'we don't like *homosexualists* round here'. I didn't get the name."

"Oh, for Christ's sake. One inaccurate media report and everybody's jumping to conclusions. And what about Dennis Iverson? What did he say?"

"He stood up for himself. They practically had to restrain him when Rupert's party came up. He said that in any case none of the villagers had been there, and that was because they hadn't been invited!"

He consulted his notebook again. "Wait, and that's not all. Another of the villagers said something like, 'Now that Iris has gone you only need to get rid of Richard Fairbairn.'"

"And how did he react?"

"He said that was ridiculous slander, of course. But he also said that in any case as the sea was advancing at a faster rate because of climate change, soon half of Blackberry Lane would be swallowed up by the waves."

Julie folded her arms and frowned. "Did you get anything directly relevant to the investigation, though?"

Bullard shook his head. "I don't think so. None of these people are suspects, are they? Shouldn't we be devoting ourselves to investigating Jeremy Iverson at this point?"

"Yes, absolutely," said Julie. She looked up as Clayton was bearing down on them.

"Reet, that's sorted then," he said. "The custody officer agrees we can hold him without charge for twenty-four hours. So, Dave, how about you follow up with Dennis Iverson, and Julie, you have another word with his wife when she comes in. Oh, and if you can, try to get hold of the sister. Wasn't Dennis Iverson going to give us her details? We'll reconvene later and pool our information before going up to see Bligh. And I'll get onto Fifi about the forensics."

"Yes guv," said Bullard and Julie in unison.

CHAPTER THIRTY-SIX

Julie was about to check the files to track down the third Iverson sibling when reception told her that Suzanna Iverson had completed her statement and was ready to leave.

"I'll be right down." She grabbed her pen and notebook and took the stairs.

She found Suzanna in her wheelchair, looking smart in a navy-blue jacket and trousers. Dange stood behind her.

"Mrs Iverson, I wonder if you could stay for a few more minutes to give me some family background? Maybe just the two of us?" she said, with a smile in the carer's direction.

"Of course. Dange, would you rather wait for me here or in the car?"

"I can go to the car." Dange held up the keys.

Julie showed Suzanna into an interview room and sat down next to her.

"How long have you had MS, if you don't mind me asking?" she began.

"Oh, I was in my early fifties when I was diagnosed. I'm lucky really, it's not the aggressive form. Just a slow but steady decline, I suppose I'd say. Anyway, what can I do for you, Detective Sergeant?"

"Could you tell me a bit about Jeremy's divorce? Was it amicable?"

"Ah," said Suzanna. *Was this a family secret?* "I wouldn't say it was an *amicable* divorce. His wife, June, took the children and accused him of unreasonable behaviour. It went to court in the end and cost Jeremy quite a lot of money, I believe."

"Do you know what sort of unreasonable behaviour?"

"I'm afraid I don't. We only heard Jeremy's side of it. It was all a long time ago." Suzanna Iverson pursed her lips. "It is what it is, as I suppose you'd say these days."

She gave a long sigh before looking down at a diamond eternity band which graced her ring finger and back up at Julie.

"I suppose I should tell you. The fact is that Jeremy isn't Dennis's child. I was two months pregnant when I met Dennis after breaking up with the father. Dennis is a most wonderful man — he brought up Jeremy as his own son. And indeed he brought him into the running of the business until all this happened."

"Did Jeremy know this? About not being your husband's son?"

"I'm afraid he did, yes. His biological father told him when he was a child, not long before Rupert was born, in fact. Jeremy had thought he was his uncle until then. It's all rather complicated, and after that his father disappeared from our lives, which was all for the best. Jeremy is only two years older than his sister Heather, so their relationship was a little closer as children. But when Rupert was born, I think Jeremy was very jealous of him. That might explain a lot of things."

Julie looked down at her notebook while she processed this. "Did you ever reveal the identity of Jeremy's father to your husband?"

The blue eyes narrowed. "I did, yes," Suzanna replied. "Not long before Rupert was born. I felt I owed it to Dennis. He was shocked of course, but he came round. It can't have been easy for him, I know . . . I should add, though, that there's no love lost between him and Jeremy's father." She gave a remorseful smile, her eyes beseeching understanding from Julie.

"Right. Now, Mr Iverson was going to let Jeremy take over the company. Do you know why he changed his mind?"

"He didn't say, really. Obviously his cancer diagnosis was weighing on his mind. You'd have to ask him, but I think he was really proud of how Rupert had succeeded with his market gardening and how the business was expanding. And also my husband respected his views on architecture and the environment. I think he believed he could make a difference if he was given the responsibility."

"Thank you very much. That's very helpful. I understand that Heather is in Northumberland?"

"Yes. She went to Durham University and basically never came back."

"I believe we have her details on record. But could you give me her phone number again so that I can check some information with her, too?"

Suzanna reached behind her for her bag which was hanging on her chair back. She produced a pen and a small notebook on which she wrote something before tearing out the page.

"That's great, thanks. What line is she in?"

"She's a speech therapist. Married to a GP in Hexham. But tell me, Detective Sergeant . . ."

"Yes?"

"Will Jeremy go to jail for murder?"

Julie had half expected the question. "It depends on lots of things. Was it premeditated? Did he intend to kill Rupert, that sort of thing. And we need evidence, obviously. Or a confession."

"Yes. Because what I've told you isn't evidence, is it?" Suzanna was fidgeting with her ring. She must be agonising over her decision to speak out, possibly fearing she'd condemned Jeremy to a murder sentence, Julie thought. And yet she owed it to Rupert's memory for his murder to be solved.

How could she come to terms with losing both her sons? Julie's heart went out to her.

"Not as such, no," Julie replied.

Suzanna wiped away tears, her slender body shaking with emotion.

Julie bent down in front of her and took her hand. "Thank you so much for coming forward. You did the right thing, Mrs Iverson. It's so important that we find out who killed your son. Now, let me show you back to your car."

* * *

Julie took a bottle of water from the drinks dispenser up to her desk where she sat, frowning at the screen. A picture was emerging of Jeremy Iverson and it wasn't pretty. She looked across the detective suite. There was no sign of either Clayton or Bullard. She picked up the phone and rang Heather Sanders. A woman with a warm and pleasant voice answered.

As soon as Julie introduced herself, Rupert's sister said, "I was wondering when I might hear from you."

CHAPTER THIRTY-SEVEN

"I'm investigating your brother's death and I need to check some family history with you," Julie explained.

"Why? Are you going to arrest someone?"

It was an odd question. Julie wondered how to reply. This call could go terribly wrong if she said too much or too little.

"It's possible that we do have a suspect, yes," she said. "I'm interested in the relationship between your two brothers."

"Who've you spoken to?"

"I just spoke to your mother."

"So you know all about our dysfunctional family then?" said Heather.

"What do you mean?"

"Welcome to the Bloomsbury set," she said with a soft laugh.

"Heather, I'm not quite sure if I understand. Your mother told me about Dennis not being Jeremy's biological father, if that's what you're talking about."

"Oh, she told you, did she?"

"Yes. I'm aware that Jeremy was jealous of Rupert when he was born, and how the two of them never got on."

"That's true enough, yes."

"But could you tell me a bit more about Jeremy? What sort of a person is he? Were you close?"

"Nobody's close to Jeremy."

"Does this go back to childhood days?" Julie asked.

"Of course. He's my big brother, and never showed any interest in me. And he was a bully. He bullied Rupert when we were young. You see, Rupert had a childhood stutter, and Jeremy and his schoolfriends mocked him terribly. Actually that's one of the reasons I trained to be a speech therapist."

"I see," said Julie. "Nobody else has mentioned Rupert's stammer to me."

"Oh, no. He got over it when he was at school, fortunately."

"Would you happen to know if this bullying trait continued into later life, for Jeremy?"

"It obviously carried on when he got married. He always had a vicious temper. I don't know why June put up with him. He beat her up — but I expect someone's told you about that already."

Julie bit back a gasp. "Really? No, your mother never mentioned it, although she did tell me about the divorce."

"Well, I only heard bits and pieces, mainly from June, but the full details obviously came out in court."

Julie wrote *family court judge* in her notebook to remind herself to ask permission to consult the court record. "By the way," she said, "I didn't see your name on the list of guests at Rupert's party. Why didn't you go?"

"Rupert invited us. But it's a long way to go, and frankly my husband didn't fancy dressing up. He didn't know anyone except Rupert. I hadn't met Cathy, although I'd heard about her. Anyway, we decided not to go. I regret it, now that he's gone . . ."

"Did you know Bethany, his ex?" Julie asked.

"Was she there?"

"Yes."

"That's good. I'm glad they stayed friends."

Julie wondered whether to spill the beans about their relationship. *Better leave that to the family*, she thought.

"I always thought they were well suited," Heather went on.

There was a pause.

"How else can I help?" Heather said.

"What about Jeremy's friends? He lives in Great Massingham, I understand."

"I don't know about friends. He's not the sort. He has acquaintances, but not friends. He's close to his birth father, mind."

Julie pressed the phone to her ear so that she didn't miss a word.

"Just a minute. I thought that he disappeared."

"So that's what Mum says, is it? He was still hanging around the place when we lived in the manor. That's why I got out as soon as I could. Dad would be out at work, and Uncle Richard would wander over and spend hours at the house."

"And did your 'Uncle Richard' continue to visit the house openly?"

"Oh, yes. Mum would sit for him. I don't know how many portraits he must have done of her over the years. And he lived nearby."

"She's a very beautiful woman." Julie was glancing back through her notebook as she spoke. Had Suzanna mentioned Jeremy's father was an artist, or that his name was Richard? She was kicking herself for not asking Suzanna outright the name of Jeremy's biological father.

"Yes. She used to be a model. Anyway, Uncle Richard wasn't the one who disappeared — it was Mum and Dad who moved to Norwich. After that, in fact, Jeremy saw a lot more of him, as far as I understand."

"So you don't think that Mr Iverson knew about the continuing relationship between Jeremy and his natural father?"

"It's possible, I suppose. But then, I wasn't there. He's devoted to my mum. I'm pretty sure that after Mum and Dad moved to Norwich, though, Uncle Richard was no longer in the picture."

"Where does he live now?" Julie asked.

"Where he's always been. At the end of Blackberry Lane. Didn't you know?"

CHAPTER THIRTY-EIGHT

Bullard and Julie sat with Clayton at his desk like three conspirators.

"OK, shoot, Julie," said Clayton. "It sounds like you may have a breakthrough here."

She looked sideways at Bullard before opening her notebook. His eyes were downcast and his lips were pursed.

She rattled through what she'd found out from Suzanna and her daughter.

"It certainly puts the animosity between Richard Fairbairn and Dennis Iverson in a new light. It's not simply about village matters," she concluded. "It goes way back."

"Here's a scenario," Clayton said. "What if Jeremy Iverson calls Richard Fairbairn that evening, leaves his parents' house in the middle of the night, picking up the keys from the hall, and drives to Tideburgh where he meets up with Richard. And the *two* of them kill Rupert?"

"So Richard would be the accomplice?" said Bullard.

"Seems plausible to me. Let's get him in. Thank God we didn't let Jeremy go."

"And the motive would be jealousy, then?" asked Bullard.

"That's right," said Julie. "Jealous of his half-brother since childhood. And he's a guy with a history of domestic violence.

He saw his chances of inheriting the family firm evaporate for ever — there was only one way he'd react. He had to get rid of the one obstacle preventing him from taking over."

Bullard gave a low whistle. "Makes sense. But Rupert was only twenty-five. That's a bit young to inherit a family firm, isn't it?"

"Louis XIV was an absolute monarch at the age of twenty-three, I seem to recall," said Julie with a smile. "And don't forget Rupert had the necessary experience and background to take over a building firm. He had a vision for the future. It sounds like Jeremy was basically a bookkeeper, despite starting out in the trade."

"Yes, that's what Dennis Iverson told me," said Bullard.

"What else did you get, Dave?" asked Clayton, swinging round.

"He confirmed that the keys to the manor are on hooks in the hall of the Norwich house. He repeated that he and his wife never heard anything during the night. When I asked if they'd hear a car on the drive, he said their bedroom is at the back of the building. So Jeremy would have been able to leave and return without being detected."

Clayton rubbed his hands. "This is promising. I'm going up to see Bligh. But we're still waiting for the damned analysis of Jeremy's DNA."

"There's another problem, guv," said Julie. "I've just remembered that Richard Fairbairn says he doesn't have a phone. He might not even be in when the uniforms go round to bring him here."

* * *

Jeremy Iverson returned to the interview room with Catherine McKinsey, who placed a thick file on the table.

Clayton reached for the recorder, glanced at Julie, and resumed the questioning.

"Can you describe your relationship with Richard Fairbairn?"

Jeremy clearly wasn't expecting the question. He froze.

Clayton leaned forward expectantly. "Mr Iverson?"

Jeremy replied, "I'm not sure what you mean. Do you mean are we friendly?"

"I believe you know exactly what I mean. What is your precise relationship with Richard Fairbairn?"

"He's my birth father."

The solicitor didn't conceal her surprise at the revelation. *She must be wondering what's coming,* Julie thought.

"And this is the Richard Fairbairn who lives on Blackberry Lane, Tideburgh, near Iverson Hall?"

"Yes." Jeremy's jaw muscles were tight.

"When was the last time you saw Mr Fairbairn?" Clayton asked.

Jeremy said nothing.

"Mr Iverson, I'd ask you to remember that this is something we can easily corroborate. Mr Fairbairn is under arrest and is on his way here. Was it on the night of Rupert's party?"

Jeremy's eyes appealed silently to his solicitor. Catherine McKinsey looked across at Julie and Clayton and said, "May I request a few minutes with my client?"

Clayton switched off the tape and they left the room.

* * *

"I say, boss, did you mean it when you said we could easily check?"

"It depends how forthcoming Richard Fairbairn is, doesn't it? He told us a pack of lies when you interviewed him the first time. Or, at least, he led us astray with his 'not me, guv' attitude. But can we use the time we have now to find out whether he really does have a phone in his name?"

"I'm on it." Julie turned to head upstairs, then added, "Kevin could probably check phone activity in the area on the party night."

"I'm going to see Kev right now, so I'll ask. I was thinking Jeremy's phone would lead us to Richard's, if he has one.

And even if he doesn't have a phone," Clayton added, "the two of them could still have arranged to meet, couldn't they?"

Julie stopped and turned to face him. "What do you mean? By sending smoke signals?"

He laughed. "We managed somehow in the old days. That must have been how they organised their sex and wigs parties in Versailles." He waved her on and turned down the corridor in search of the IT chief.

* * *

A few minutes later the detectives reassembled in the interview room with Jeremy Iverson and his solicitor. Would Catherine McKinsey have persuaded him to be more cooperative?

Clayton switched on the tape again, with a glance up at the blinking light on the video monitor in the corner. Julie presumed that Bligh was watching the proceedings from her desk upstairs.

"Mr Iverson, the question was, when did you last see your biological father, Richard Fairbairn?" Clayton began.

"It was on the night of the party," said Jeremy. Julie felt a wave of relief wash over her.

Clayton followed up. "And did the two of you go to Iverson Hall with the intention of murdering Rupert Iverson?"

Jeremy took a deep breath. Speaking slowly and deliberately, he replied, "No, we did not. We went to the house in order to persuade him not to accept my father's offer of taking over the business."

"But why the urgency? Couldn't it have waited?"

"It *was* urgent. From what my mother said that night, Rupert was going to give his answer the next day."

"Was Mr Fairbairn expecting you? Please tell us what happened."

"Well, on Saturday nights I usually meet up with Richard in a pub somewhere. But we couldn't do that on the night of the party because I was with my mother. He rang me from a pub in Wymondham at about ten and asked if I could join him and a friend. I couldn't, obviously, because I was with my mother. But I told him about our conversation. He was as angry as I was."

"We understand that his relations with Mr Iverson aren't particularly friendly," said Julie.

Jeremy looked at her as though she'd interrupted his train of thought. "That's true. That's because of his property being at risk of falling into the sea, among other issues."

"Other issues? Please clarify, Mr Iverson."

"You're aware of the racket from the parties at Iverson Hall? The neighbours can't get to sleep at night," he replied.

"Do continue." Clayton threw a sideways glance at Julie. "What did Mr Fairbairn say on the phone then?"

"He said he was going home. We agreed that we needed to persuade Rupert to refuse. So I said I'd join him in Tideburgh and we'd go to see Rupert together."

"And what time did you do that?" Clayton asked.

"I left the house at about 2 a.m. so I got there about forty-five minutes later, I suppose."

"You took the keys to the manor with you?" Julie interjected.

"Yes. My father keeps them in the hall."

"You didn't attempt to phone Rupert before you left, or message him?"

"No. I thought he'd be busy with the party. And anyway, like I said, Richard and I decided it would be better if we both went to the house, to talk to him in person."

"Why was that?" Clayton asked.

Jeremy seemed to be casting around for an explanation. "Two of us might have a better chance of . . . persuading him. And one of us needed to wait downstairs to be on the lookout, in case anyone from the party was wandering around at 3 a.m. We didn't want random people listening in to our private conversation."

"So you went in the front door? And then what?"

"Yes. Richard waited at the bottom of the stairs and I was going to go up to Rupert's room. But I got a bit of a shock when we almost bumped into each other on the stairs. He had this wig on and his costume, and at first I thought I'd seen a ghost. We both jumped. He said he was going to get some water from the kitchen. I said, 'Happy birthday.' He asked me what the hell I was doing there. I told him to be quiet and that we had some private business to discuss."

"And he cooperated?"

"Yes. I said it was about the firm. He came with us to the summer house because it would be quiet. He said he was going to accept his father's proposal and that he intended to tell him in the morning. He said he had big plans, that he wanted to make big changes at Iverson and Son. It sounded like he'd already agreed a lot with my father without even consulting me — after all I'd done for the company! At that point Richard picked up the broom."

Clayton's phone pinged. He looked down at the message and back at Jeremy Iverson. Julie wondered if it could be the forensics result they'd been waiting for, but Clayton's face was expressionless.

"You decided to beat some sense into him?"

"To be honest, we didn't exactly plan how we'd force him to change his mind. But when Richard picked up the broom, Rupert lunged at him and fought back. Then I joined in. I got angry, I pushed him, and he pushed me back and the two of us began fighting. I looked for something and saw the cricket bat." Jeremy stopped abruptly.

"Please continue, Mr Iverson," said Clayton.

Jeremy glanced again at the solicitor. "I hit Rupert on the head and I realised I'd hurt him as he fell onto the cushions. But then he sat up and he was even angrier. He said he wasn't going to work with me, not after I'd attacked him."

"So what happened then?" Julie asked.

"We took him to the pool to see whether he'd change his mind after a dunking."

"A dunking? Whose idea was that?" Clayton asked.

"Both of us," said Jeremy, again glancing at the lawyer. "There was a bit of pushing and shoving. All three of us ended up in the pool, in the shallow end."

"Then what happened?"

"After we'd pushed his head down a couple of times, Rupert was spluttering and we realised he wouldn't back down, so we left him there, in the pool."

"You attacked him and left him in the pool," said Clayton. "Did you not think that he'd have called for help and accused you of the attack?"

"Oh. We'd thought about that," said Jeremy after a pause.

"Please continue."

"We warned him that if he spoke to anyone we'd hurt his girlfriend . . . we might have threatened an acid attack."

"You might have threatened? Or you did threaten?"

"OK. We threatened. We wouldn't have actually done it. And that proves that we didn't intend to kill him, doesn't it? We only wanted to teach him a lesson."

Julie and Clayton exchanged a look. Threatening to disfigure Bethany with an acid attack? How sick was that?

"What was the name of Rupert's girlfriend?" Julie asked.

"Cathy, of course," said Jeremy, seemingly surprised by the question.

Oh God, Julie thought. *These jokers weren't even threatening the right woman.* But Rupert wouldn't have wanted either woman to be hurt, so the threat would have been powerful.

"What was Rupert's response to that?" Clayton asked.

"I don't recall him saying anything. We'd made our point."

"And then what happened? You were all soaking wet," said Julie, remembering Jeremy's trousers.

"Yes. We got out of the pool and went back to the summer house because we realised we needed to get rid of the cricket bat and broom."

"You left by the back entrance?"

"Yes. Over the gate. Then we chucked the bat off the cliff as we could hear the waves below." At the mention of the cricket bat, Clayton turned ever so slightly towards Julie who understood immediately why his phone had pinged. "Richard took the broom home with him, he thought it would be safe," Jeremy continued.

"And what about your clothes?"

"Richard gave me some clean trousers as mine were wet. I left them at his place and he gave them back a few days later." So that would explain why Suzanna noticed that Jeremy's trousers were too large — they weren't even his, thought Julie.

"Now, Mr Fairbairn had been drinking. Was he drunk?" she asked.

"You'll have to ask him. He'd been at the pub so he wasn't stone-cold sober."

"And what about you?"

"I had a glass of wine with my mother over dinner. I might have had two, but I wasn't drunk, no," said Jeremy. "Although we did have a beer or two at Richard's place before we walked round to the house."

"Did either of you realise that you'd killed Rupert?"

"Of course not! We thought that he might think twice after we punished him about taking over the firm. I already told you that."

"Jeremy Iverson," Clayton said, "I am charging you with the murder of Rupert Iverson. You do not have to say anything but it may harm your defence if you do not mention now something that you later rely on in court. Anything you do say may be given in evidence."

Jeremy said nothing. He looked lost.

CHAPTER THIRTY-NINE

Clayton and Julie waited in the interview room while the custody officer finished with Richard Fairbairn.

"Lucky coincidence about that text," said Julie. "Was it about the bat?"

"Yes," said Clayton. "It was Bligh saying she'd got the OK from the CPS to charge him even before the confirmation from forensics came through with a match to Jeremy's DNA. But McKinsey must also have talked some sense into him. He clearly thought he could get away with it until we mentioned Richard Fairbairn."

"The bottom line is that neither of them helped Rupert out of the pool. They left him there for dead," said Julie. "They got rid of the bat — so even if he was alive when they walked away, it's obvious they knew they'd left him for dead. And they had a plan, even the threat against the girlfriend. It was a premeditated attack, even if they didn't intend to kill him."

"Yes. We'll see if Richard Fairbairn has a different recollection about whose idea it was to dunk him." Clayton looked at his watch. "How much longer do they need? We could have had a cup of tea by now."

The door opened, and Richard Fairbairn came in, accompanied by a duty solicitor. Richard was slightly dishevelled and scowling. *What on earth did Suzanna Iverson ever see in him? Maybe she liked a bit of rough.* By Julie's calculations, he would have been in his early twenties when Jeremy was born. Suzanna was a few years older than him. She'd kept the love of two men over decades. *Now one son has been murdered by her former lover.*

Julie felt a pang of sympathy for the older woman. She presumably had no idea of Richard's involvement.

Clayton had turned on the tape and reminded Richard of his rights and that he'd been arrested on suspicion of the murder of Rupert Iverson.

"Mr Fairbairn, whose idea was it to go round to Iverson Manor in the middle of the night?" Clayton asked.

"I don't recall," he replied. "I invited Jeremy over to my place because he was naturally upset that his life might be about to be ruined. We realised that all we had to do was to persuade Rupert to turn down his father's offer. Jeremy told me that Rupert was going to give his answer the next day."

"Right. But why did you go to Iverson Hall at that time of night?" Clayton continued. "It looks like you were cooking up a plan."

"It had to be so late because, number one, Jeremy had to leave the house in Norwich without Dennis Iverson finding out. And number two, we didn't want to arrive while the party was in full flow because Jeremy wanted a private conversation with Rupert."

"But if he wanted a private conversation, why did you go along?" Julie interjected.

"Because Jeremy asked me," Richard flung back. "Blood is thicker than water, you know."

He looked at the lawyer before adding, "He thought Rupert might pay more attention if there were two of us."

"So here you are leaving your bungalow. Which way did you go to the house? Across the paddock?"

"No. We went along Blackberry Lane and down the road. We wanted to make sure the party had finished and that the lights were off. There were three cars parked outside. One was Rupert's and we thought the two others belonged to guests who were staying the night. Jeremy had the keys to the house, and we went in through the front door."

"Then what?"

"I waited in the hall. Jeremy went up to fetch Rupert, who wandered down in his party costume. He said he was getting a drink of water from the kitchen. We persuaded him to go down to the summer house for privacy."

"And how did the conversation go?" Julie asked.

"Rupert made it clear that he'd no intention of turning down his dad's offer. In fact, the way he was talking, it almost sounded like Jeremy was going to be pushed out — Rupert and his father must have been making decisions behind his back already. Jeremy reacted to that and there was some pushing and shoving. I picked up whatever I could lay my hands on and we decided to teach him a lesson. We thought maybe he'd change his mind."

"But did he?" Clayton asked.

"No."

"And after you pushed him with the broom, Jeremy Iverson picked up a cricket bat, correct?"

"Yes. Rupert was fighting back. But after Jeremy hit him with the bat, he still hadn't changed his mind about taking over the firm. Actually, he said then that he wanted Jeremy out — he wouldn't work with him after the fight they'd just had."

"So then what did you do?" Clayton asked.

"We dunked him in the pool."

Julie was struck by the use of the same language by both of the attackers.

"Which one of you decided?" she asked.

"Both of us," he replied, after a pause. Julie wondered which one of the two was covering for the other. They'd had plenty of time to agree a story, after all.

Richard gave an identical account to Jeremy's about Rupert's water torture.

"Mr Fairbairn, the pathologist's report describes the fatal injuries sustained by Rupert Iverson as tantamount to waterboarding. What's your response to that?" Clayton asked.

"Like I said, we never intended to kill him. We just wanted to teach him a lesson." Richard was again using the same language as Jeremy Iverson.

Julie intervened. "Mr Fairbairn, you told us earlier that you'd found the broom on the beach a few days after the murder. This seems to be rather strange because it could easily have been picked up by our forensics team before then. Do you stand by that statement?"

Richard shifted in his seat and ran his thick fingers through his hair. "You're right. I took it home," he said. "It was the cricket bat that we threw into the sea."

"You concealed a weapon used in the attack and then tried to wash off the evidence. Why did you take it to your home?" Julie pressed him.

He glanced at his lawyer. "Well, I figured that you wouldn't have a reason to search my home."

"And did Mr Iverson accompany you to your home?"

"Yes he did. He needed a dry pair of trousers, so I gave him some jeans and then he went back to Norwich."

"How much had you had to drink that night, Mr Fairbairn?"

"A fair bit, I suppose," he replied. "It was Saturday night, after all. I had a few beers at the Green Dragon with my friend. After he dropped me off, I had two or three more while I waited for Jeremy. We each had one after he arrived."

"And what about Jeremy? Was he under the influence?"

"He was driving. I wouldn't say so, no. He didn't seem drunk to me."

"We'll need the details of the friend you were drinking with at the Green Dragon," said Clayton. He closed his file, read out the identical murder charge against Richard Fairbairn that he'd used against Jeremy Iverson, switched off the tape and stood up.

CHAPTER FORTY

Clayton and Julie took the lift straight up to Bligh's office. She was expecting them.

"That went well," she said. "It's pretty clear that they're going down together. I don't think we could say one was the accomplice; they're both responsible. They left him for dead in the pool and they chucked away the murder weapon."

"Well, Fairbairn was pretty far gone, apparently. And it was three o'clock in the morning. What on earth were the pair of them thinking?" said Clayton.

"Jeremy has a history of violence, remember," said Julie. "He obviously lashes out instead of thinking things through. And Fairbairn has his own personal vendetta against Dennis Iverson. Little did we know how far back their enmity went."

"Maybe they originally intended to beat him up, but Jeremy obviously lost it after Rupert said he didn't want him in the firm anymore."

"And as far as Fairbairn was concerned, he was up for it because blood is thicker than water," said Julie.

The three of them fell silent for a moment as though marking the end of the investigation. Julie remembered what Heather Sanders had said about Jeremy mistreating Rupert over his stammer. It was obvious that the pair of them would never have been able to work together in the family firm.

"Well done, both of you," said Bligh. Clayton and Julie got up to go, but Bligh called Julie back.

"Thank you for your report on Marianne Andrews," she said. "Could you pop in to see me tomorrow once these two have appeared in court?"

"Yes, ma'am," said Julie, and followed Clayton down the stairs.

"Do you fancy a cuppa?" she asked him, as they entered the detective suite.

"I was thinking of something stronger, myself. It's been a long day, hasn't it? What about the Green Dragon?"

Julie checked her watch. It was 6.30 p.m. She realised that Ollie would be home alone after football practice. She'd have to call in a favour from her next-door neighbour.

"Sure, why not?" she said. "Shall we pick up Dave?"

* * *

The three detectives parked in the car park behind the black-and-white-striped Market Cross at the heart of Wymondham village. They walked down to the Green Dragon against a blustery wind and light rain.

"Any particular reason we're drinking here?" Julie asked, as its medieval exterior came into view.

"Of course." Clayton winked at her. "What a pity the pub garden's not open."

They went inside and found a corner table under the dark wooden beams in the front room. "What's your poison?" Clayton asked. "It's on me."

"G and T please," said Julie.

"Pint of bitter please," said Bullard. "Green Dragon."

The pub was beginning to fill up with a young after-work crowd. The noise level around them was rising. Julie looked over towards the bar and saw Clayton in conversation with the landlord. He returned with the drinks and threw down a packet of crisps and some pork scratchings onto the table. The three of them clinked their glasses.

"Well?" Julie asked Clayton. "Did you get what you came for?"

He nodded. "The landlord confirms that Richard Fairbairn is one of the regulars. So is Jeremy Iverson. He doesn't remember the night of the party specifically, but on Saturday nights he says that Richard doesn't half put them away."

"I noticed that the first time I went to his place. There were loads of beer cans behind him when he opened the door. He looks like a heavy drinker, doesn't he?"

"Jeremy's lucky living in Great Massingham. He's probably got one of the best pubs in Norfolk in his village," said Bullard.

"The Dabbling Duck?"

"That's right." Bullard smiled. "I was hoping we'd have to question him at home one evening."

They sipped their drinks, enjoying the rare companionship out of hours. It certainly made a change from the cafeteria at the nick.

"Families, eh?" said Clayton, out of nowhere, shaking his head. Julie had the sense that he was including his own. She smiled inwardly as she imagined him driving round with his father's ashes in the car boot.

"I feel sorry for that family, particularly Suzanna. She's lost both of her sons now, hasn't she, as well as Jeremy's birth father. What a disaster." Julie took a sip of her drink and stared into the glass.

"If she hadn't said anything to you, though, she'd surely have regretted it," suggested Bullard. "Jeremy might have literally got away with murder, and she'd have that on her conscience for the rest of her life."

"True enough," said Clayton. "Anyway, well done, both of you. We cracked it."

"It was down to Julie," said Bullard.

"Thanks, but it was touch and go, wasn't it? It was a lucky break we had," she said.

"That's often the way, isn't it?" Clayton looked around the bar. "But I don't know whether I'll ever get to understand what goes on in the villages round here. This one had everything, fear and loathing, lust, jealousy . . . you name it."

"Not to mention sex and wigs," Julie added. They all laughed. "The press are going to have a field day with this one, once they figure out the family relationships. Poor old Dennis Iverson. Wait till he hears it was his wife's ex-lover who killed his son."

"I've been thinking about Bethany's surprise," said Bullard. "It must be that Rupert was going to say 'yes' to Dennis's offer. If he'd told her on the night of the party, or even made an announcement, I wonder if things might have turned out quite differently."

Julie remembered what Jeremy had said about obtaining Rupert's silence by threatening Cathy, not Bethany. She wondered if they really would have carried out an acid attack. What a tragic case of mistaken identity that would have been.

They sat back, savouring the moment. The successful conclusion of an investigation with its ups and downs was always such a relief. Julie looked at her watch. She'd have to go home to Ollie in a few minutes.

"So what have you both got planned for tonight?" Clayton asked.

"Nothing exciting," she replied. "Mac and cheese with my boy. I've put the fear of God into him about pulling his weight around the house. With a bit of luck he might have grated the cheese."

"Sounds nice," said Bullard. "It's my turn to make sure the girls do their homework. What about you, Sam?"

"I've got a date," he said with a big grin.

Clayton rarely mentioned his private life, so Julie asked, "You're back together again, then?"

"Yes. How did you guess?"

"I wondered why you've been so cheerful since you got back." She put her glass down. "Anyway . . ." And they understood she was leaving.

"Same again?" Clayton asked Bullard.

"Why not?" he said. Julie got up and left them to it.

* * *

Julie had to wait until the following afternoon to find out what Bligh wanted to talk to her about. Earlier, the detectives had gathered round a TV to watch the DCI handle the press conference. The crime reporter from the *Eastern Daily Press* peppered her with follow-up questions. She praised their major investigation team for securing the confessions from the two suspects. But Julie found herself regretting they hadn't pressed Richard Fairbairn earlier when he'd been questioned. They'd had to wait until the chance discovery of his relationship with Suzanna and Jeremy to crack open the case.

She was glad that Bligh didn't mention Suzanna's role in the outcome and wondered how she and her husband were coping. Jeremy's parentage certainly hadn't stopped Dennis from involving him in the family business and naming it Iverson and Son. But it was clear that Rupert had always been Dennis's favourite child.

Julie remembered the portrait of Suzanna, hanging proudly in the Iverson's home. Had it been painted by 'Uncle Richard'? For Dennis Iverson, the picture would be a permanent reminder of the tragedy that had befallen their family during the little time that he had left to live.

She returned to her desk and began clearing away the Post-it notes from her computer screen. As she was about to get up for a drink of water, her phone rang.

Bligh swivelled round to face her when she knocked on her door, and gestured to a chair.

"Congratulations, Julie. I've been very impressed by your handling of this case in Sam's absence," she said.

"Thank you, ma'am. It was teamwork."

"Tell me, you've been in Norwich for more than two years, haven't you?"

"Just over three, I believe, ma'am."

"Yes. Tell me, where do you see yourself going, in terms of policing?"

"I'd like to lead investigations, if that's what you mean. More responsibility. Yes, definitely."

"Good. Because I'm minded to recommend you for temporary promotion to DI while the assessment is carried out. You've more than proved your competence in your current rank."

Julie had been surprised by Bligh's fulsome praise and certainly hadn't expected this.

"Gosh," she said. "Thank you."

"There's the exam, of course, but you're used to that sort of pressure, aren't you?"

Julie smiled and nodded. She was speechless.

* * *

Julie stood at the door of the detective suite. Clayton was at his workstation. Had he had anything to do with this?

She spread her fingers out in front of her and examined the backs of her hands, still blemished by weals and dry patches. It was time to look to the future. She resolved that the very first thing she was going to do was to book an appointment with a therapist to deal with her OCD once and for all.

She walked over to Clayton to ask if he needed her for anything.

"No, you can head off if you like."

"OK, I will. Thank you. I mean, thanks for everything."

He grinned at her and gave her a wink. Then she picked up her bag and set off for home. With a bit of luck she might be there before Ollie.

She drove back to Costessey, checked twice that she'd put the handbrake on before opening the front door, and saw that Ollie's jacket was hanging on a peg in the hall. She went into the kitchen where she saw a neatly diced onion on a plate and sliced carrots in a pan of water.

Then she rushed upstairs to his bedroom where he was seated at his computer. She pulled him up, opened her arms wide and wrapped him in a bear hug as she danced him round the room to the rhythm of his video game.

THE END

ACKNOWLEDGEMENTS

This novel was inspired by the spectacle of the collapsing cliffs in and around the Norfolk village of Happisburgh. I wish to thank the landlord of the listed Hill House Inn in Happisburgh, District Councillor Clive Stockton. He made me fully aware of the plight of villagers living in North Norfolk coastal communities where the sea is destroying cliffside homes, livelihoods and the local heritage. His home and business, where he and his wife Sue have lived for thirty years, is under threat from the accelerating coastal erosion. I'm indebted once again to former police officer Robert Erett for sharing his expertise. My thanks also go to my critical readers for their frank and invaluable feedback, particularly my long-suffering friends Margaret Crompton, Charles Kaye, Mary Friel and Mike Gray. They know that sometimes I need saving from myself. I'm grateful to two other lovely friends, actor Holly Rose Clegg, who featured in a TV series about Louis XIV, and Alex Frean, who unwittingly helped me across the finish line with their fresh insights.

With thanks, as ever, to my brilliant editors at Joffe Books. Any mistakes of course are mine alone.

ALSO BY ANNE PENKETH

DI CLAYTON MYSTERIES
Book 1: MURDER ON THE MARSH
Book 2: THE BAD SISTER
Book 3: PLAY DEAD
Book 4: MURDER AT THE MANOR

Thank you for reading this book.

If you enjoyed it please leave feedback on Amazon or Goodreads, and if there is anything we missed or you have a question about, then please get in touch. We appreciate you choosing our book.

Founded in 2014 in Shoreditch, London, we at Joffe Books pride ourselves on our history of innovative publishing. We were thrilled to be shortlisted for Independent Publisher of the Year at the British Book Awards.

www.joffebooks.com

We're very grateful to eagle-eyed readers who take the time to contact us. Please send any errors you find to corrections@joffebooks.com. We'll get them fixed ASAP.

Printed in Dunstable, United Kingdom

66735751R00129